Madman

Joseph Pesavento

Copyright © 2021 by Joseph Pesavento

All rights reserved.

No part of this publication may be reproduced, distributed, or transmitted in any form or by any means, including photocopying, recording, or other electronic or mechanical methods, without the prior written permission of the publisher, except as permitted by U.S. copyright law. For permission requests, contact Joseph Pesavento.

The story, all names, characters, and incidents portrayed in this production are fictitious. No identification with actual persons (living or deceased), places, buildings, and products is intended or should be inferred.

ISBN: 9798734256596

Book Cover design by Mitch Green of Rad Publishing.

Editing and Formatting for second edition by Candace Nola of 360 Editing, (a division of Uncomfortably Dark Horror).

Second Edition 2024

www.josephpesavento.com

Dedication

To Father, may my words be devoted to your legacy.

To Mother, you've guided me from all the darkness I've faced.

To Nadia, you've made the light sempiternal.

Contents

1. A Grim Discovery — 1
2. Where We Meet — 3
3. Street Kids — 9
4. While Sleeping — 23
5. Orb — 28
6. Pet — 42
7. Gone, Mother — 46
8. The Last Time I Saw You — 50
9. I Love This City — 55
10. Final Angel — 65
11. Where To Go To Feel Nothing — 73
12. Feeding — 87
13. All Was Quiet — 94
14. The Last Snowfall — 109

15. Heat Form	121
16. I Saw Her Floating	137
17. What They Left Behind	147
18. Return From The Depths	160
19. A Final Clue	181
20. Keep It In The Family	182
Acknowledgements	193
About the author	195

1

A Grim Discovery

ON THE MORNING OF JULY 9th, AUTHORITIES FOUND A DEAD BODY, WHICH REMAINS UNIDENTIFIED, IN AN ABANDONED BUILDING. THE UNIDENTIFIED MALE SLASHED HIS WRISTS TO THE POINT OF BEING ALMOST SEVERED. BESIDE HIM WERE SEVERAL PILES OF LINED PAPER, CAREFULLY STACKED AND SORTED. IN HIS CLENCHED FIST WAS HIS SUICIDE NOTE.

I'VE HEARD THEM SPEAKING to me for several years now. Each year, they grow louder and more detailed about what they see, what they do, and what they experience. A man can only absorb so much death before he craves it himself. I've had my taste, and now I only want death more. I starve for it.

The voices are never quiet. They repeat the horrors they face, and now they've become my horrors.

I wanted to die, but they wouldn't let me until I'd heard every word.

I've written it all down. May these words aid you in understanding what happened to me. I hope they can save someone else.

They didn't save me.

Goodbye.

2

Where We Meet

It was the exact spot where they met every weekend, right by the park near their old high school. They'd been doing this since they graduated. Seven years ago, to the day. It was odd to reflect on how long it'd been. Nearly a decade of a trivial tradition, yet it overwhelms Jeremy when they can't meet.

Jeremy waited for Sophia as he usually does. It's rare for her to be on time, but tonight is especially unusual for her. She's over an hour late—no call or text. He reached out but heard nothing. It's creepy in the park where Jeremy stands alone.

Another half-hour goes by. Jeremy calls her, but he seems to have no service. Weird. This isn't normal. Another fifteen minutes. He texts her to see if everything is okay. No answer. Jeremy gets worried.

However, something is pulling his attention away from the seldom-punctual friend of his. Tires screech, sounding as if they are right behind Jeremy. He looks around and sees nothing. There isn't a car in sight for as far as he can see. The situation is getting weirder and weirder.

Suddenly, Jeremy felt a touch on his shoulder. He recognizes the touch. It's her.

"Don't turn around," Sophia says abruptly.

"Are you okay? I've been trying to get ahold of you," asks Jeremy.

"No. I'm not."

Jeremy tries to turn, but she applies pressure to his shoulder.

"Please, let me see you," Jeremy begs. She doesn't seem to budge. This isn't like her, so he suspects something unusual happened.

"Sophia."

Her grip loosened. Jeremy felt her hand slide away from his shoulder. It scared him to turn around and see what he didn't know yet. She was never like this; Jeremy never felt like this.

He turned around to face her. Her smile spread across her face as wide as he'd ever seen. Her teeth were glowing, and she stared at Jeremy like she hadn't seen him in years. He smiled back at her. The moment was unlike anything they'd had before. Then Jeremy noticed the blood that poured from her hairline, dripping down the side of her face.

"Sophia, what happened? You're bleeding!" Jeremy yelled out.

She touched her face and felt the blood. She looked down at her fingers, drenched in red.

"You don't remember?"

"What? Remember what?" Jeremy asked. "The crash."

Jeremy couldn't grasp what she'd said. What crash? He felt uncomfortable, and she kept making him so frightened. Here is Sophia, right in front of Jeremy, like any other time before. Yet she's bleeding as if someone had hit her with a bat, and she's maintaining her composure. Is she lying? Am I dreaming this? I'm losing grip on what reality I know, or at least thought I knew. Thoughts raced through Jeremy's head.

"Sophia, what crash?"

"The car crash," she said calmly.

Jeremy heard it again. The tires screeched much louder this time. It echoed around them, yet Sophia barely seemed to notice it.

"Did you hear that sound?" Jeremy asked.

She said nothing, but worked up a smile. That's when he realized what had happened.

"The crash... it only just happened."

"Yes," she said.

What she described was overwhelming. Tonight was supposed to be routine, like any other night. Jeremy and Sophia were supposed to talk like they always do, walk to the store and get their usual potato chips and energy drinks, and walk back to talk about anything that was on their minds. There were never supposed to be any alterations, no backup plans, and no cancellations. Yet here he was, standing before Sophia, and she has an injury from a crash. The strange thing is how calm she is after all of this.

"Listen, Sophia. I think you're a little confused. You were just in a serious accident," Jeremy said.

The sound came again, this time as loud as an arena filled with thousands of people. The sound made Jeremy's knees buckle. He covered his ears to help stop the ringing that rattled his brain until it felt as if it were about to burst at any second. He can't stand. The noise is genuinely overwhelming, to the point it makes him scream back at it. Jeremy looks up at Sophia to see how she's coping with this noise. She reacts as if it were nothing but a faint raise in volume.

"How can you not hear that?" Jeremy asked.

"I was already dead before the sound came," Sophia said.

"What are you talking about?" Jeremy asked.

After several minutes of utter confusion at how trivial she was making this whole situation out to be, she finally said the words that Jeremy didn't want to hear, but needed to.

"The oncoming car hit my side and threw me several feet. I landed hard on my head, making me bleed to death. You died when the car hit the tree, pinning you in between," Sophia said.

Before Jeremy could react, his face began to feel warm. As if someone was patting his face with a damp, warm cloth. It was blood gushing down from the top of his head. It ran over his right eye and down his cheek. He wiped and wiped, but it never seemed to stop. Jeremy felt his shirt sticking out near his right side and was shocked to see several ribs poking through the shirt. He couldn't remember what he wore today, with the blood staining and leaking through his shirt. It slowly began to make more sense.

They weren't alive.

In some other state that Jeremy couldn't define, they were still themselves, seconds out of the crash that killed them. More blood poured from Jeremy's head, and he touched near his hairline to find a gash that reached his skull. He felt nothing when he touched it. It's possible he was dead, but he couldn't grasp how eerie this calming sensation was.

"Can you feel anything?" Jeremy asked. "Anything at all?"

"No," Sophia said.

Jeremy noticed a spot of blood expanding on her side. It grew larger with every second. She saw he was staring and began to look.

"I don't feel it at all," Sophia said.

"How are you not even remotely distraught about all of this?" Jeremy asked.

"It's simple," Sophia said. "I was right where I needed to be."

"What do you mean?" Jeremy asked, still stunned at the wonder of her composure.

"We were where we met every single weekend. Right by the park near our high school. We've been doing this since we graduated seven years ago."

She was right. She knew it just like Jeremy did. This is what we were supposed to be doing, and where we were supposed to be. Someone who'd had a little too much to drink had other plans for the two of them.

"Look," Sophia said.

Jeremy turned around to see the driver slowly exiting his car. He was stunned to see their corpses in the positions that Sophia had so graphically described. Jeremy had a hard time seeing his dead body, but felt closure upon witnessing it. The driver was hardly injured. There was a cut or two on his face, and what looked like a broken arm. He assessed the damages to his car and began to walk away.

"Where is he going?" Jeremy asked. "I'm not sure," Sophia said.

He began to pick up speed. He looked back and started to run.

"He's leaving us," Jeremy said. "Just abandoning us to rot in the street."

"No, he isn't," she said. "We are right where we need to be."

Sophia looked at Jeremy and smiled.

The situation was too far-fetched to accept. Jeremy is now beyond the living. His family and friends will never see him again. Yet, knowing that Sophia was with him during this fatal incident, he felt at ease. He went out tonight doing what he was supposed to do, and now he can do it forever, with her.

Jeremy smiled back at her.

"Okay," Jeremy said. "To the park we go."

They walked into the dark, past their mangled bodies and the car that had ended the life they'd always known. Jeremy and Sophia entered the park that they've visited regularly for the better half of a decade.

Tonight is another night for them to remember forever.

3

Street Kids

Greg rushed into the garage with a burst of confidence. He grabbed his helmet and strapped it on, making sure it fit comfortably. He jumped on his bike and pedaled to the end of the driveway. Today is the day he's waited and planned for. Today, he would conquer the hill of all hills.

"Hold it!" Greg's mother screamed. "Did you plan on telling me you're going off on your bike?"

"Yes, Mom. I was just riding it out of the garage then I was going to tell you. I'm going over to Lee's. His dad just bought him a ramp for his driveway," Greg said.

"What time are you getting home?" she asked. Greg always hated this question. Lee lived no more than two blocks away. Lee's mom was a stay-at-home mom, so she was always there unless she went grocery shopping on weekends while Lee's dad slept in from his grueling work hours. Greg rolled his eyes and answered every time, because anything less than that wouldn't get him out of the house at all.

"Mom, I have my cell phone. Just call or text me. I'll be gone for a few hours," Greg said. He held back every urge to yell out how ridiculous she was being. "And yes, I'll be careful."

"Okay. Please tell Lee's parents I said hello. Have fun!" Greg's mom said.

Greg was so eager to get on with his lie that he didn't bother to say goodbye to his mom. Sure, she might find out that her son wasn't going down the street to his friend's house. She didn't know Lee's dad hadn't bought him a new ramp. She also didn't know that Greg didn't really like Lee that much. He only spent time with Lee in a large group of friends, or whenever Lee actually did get something new because Lee often got things the other kids couldn't afford.

Greg knew his mom would kill him if she found out he'd went to try a dangerous bike stunt rather than stay close to the house, but no kid in school had dominated this hill and he was confident he could take it on today. Every kid in school would think he was a legend if he managed to take this hill.

After a ten-minute ride down Main Street, a quick pass down Lattintown Road, and flying down Orchard Avenue right past the police station, Greg stopped at the base of Bloom Street. To the locals, it was referred to as "Doom and Gloom Hill". It had a dark history of high schoolers crashing their cars at the many intersections, and Greg's parents always told him stories of kids who were hit by cars when they were kids themselves. He didn't believe them.

Another lie to keep me from doing anything fun, Greg thought.

Greg looked up at the steep hill. It was a straight ride all the way down if he could avoid any cars taking him out. At least four intersections created an obstacle for him, but he knew there wasn't normally traffic during this time of day, in this part of town. It was a heavily residential area, so most people were either home or out of town for the weekend. Still, Greg needed a witness if he was going to succeed with this. He pulled out his phone and dialed Brandon's number.

"Brandon, can you meet me at Doom and Gloom?" Greg asked.

"Hey, Greg. If my mom lets me out. What's going on?" Brandon asked.

"I'm doing it today. I'm heading up now," Greg said. He couldn't hold back his smile.

"Wait, really? Holy shit! I'm coming now. MOM! Can I-" Brandon said before being cut off by Greg.

Greg made his slow ascension up, pedaling hard. He learned quickly this hill was harder going up than down. He hopped off his bike and pushed it up the hill to save energy. He passed the first intersection with ease. Only one car passed when he was walking up and he grew more excited there would be few obstacles standing in the way of completing his stunt.

The second stretch after the first intersection was much steeper than the first. Greg breathed intensely while pushing his bike. He dropped his bike down and tried to catch his breath. He leaned over, not paying attention to his surroundings. Two feet walked in front of him, and he looked up to see a kid holding his helmet, standing on the other side of the street. His face was pale and his pupils seemed gray. The pale boy waved at Greg.

"Hey, what's up?" Greg asked, waving with a little effort as his lungs were still recovering.

"Hey, are you going to do the hill?" the boy asked.

"Yeah. It's tough walking up to it, though. I'm going to take my time," Greg said. "Are you new around here?"

"No. I tried this hill once. Didn't get very far. Anyway, good luck!" the boy said. He turned to walk away, and Greg noticed a large chunk of his head was missing in the back. Part of his brain dangled down by his neck, and the back of his shirt was soaked in blood. He walked down the street and slowly faded into nothing.

Greg was too startled to say anything—if what he saw was actually real. *I must be getting light-headed,* he thought. Greg grabbed his bike and walked up a little further, making sure to pace himself this time.

After clearing the second half of the steep hill, Greg collapsed again. He dropped his bike and wiped the sweat collecting under his helmet and on his forehead. *This hill better be worth the trouble,* he thought. Greg knelt down, as he couldn't find breathing easier standing up. He thought this hill would defeat him before he even got to the top.

"Holy crap, this hill is steep," Greg said in between breaths.

"Yeah, I remember how long it took me to climb up all those years ago. I think I took a thirty-minute break right at the bottom of that last steep stretch. Those were some great memories," a young girl said, appearing like the creepy little gruesome boy from before. She flipped her hair back and Greg noticed her neck moved unusually.

"Who are you? Where did you come from?" Greg asked. He stared at her movements, focusing on her eerily-free neck.

"I'm Megan. I rode down this hill about twenty-three years ago. Almost made it to the bottom, too. If only that car wasn't driving so fast," Megan said. "My head went through the windshield, but my body stayed on the hood. Died right away."

"Did you just say... You're dead?" Greg asked.

Now the little boy didn't seem so off to Greg. Megan moved her hair again, revealing a slit crossing near her necklace. She smiled at him and he stared at her neck movements. It moved with ease, like a tree branch about to snap with a strong gust of wind.

"Yeah. It's a shame because so many people thought I could do the hill. I mean, I really tried! That's how life is, I guess. I wish my parents didn't have to deal with all that grief, though," Megan said.

Greg was at a loss for words. *Was the heat getting to his head? Were these mysteriously injured kids a part of his exhaustion?* Maybe this was the voice in the back of his head, telling him not to go through with it or he'll end up like these two. He didn't want to believe it, but it was as if she were like any other girl standing right across from him. He couldn't focus on anything besides the slit in her neck, so he stood up with a plan to test her.

"If you're really dead, why don't you show me the slit in your neck? I think you're just trying to scare me," Greg said.

Megan smiled. "That's silly. I don't even know you. It's pretty cool if you look at it close."

Megan tilted her head down and pulled further at the opposite side of her head. A slit from her right shoulder, reaching across her collarbone, exposed a fleshy mass. Broken bone poked out when she leaned further. Greg could only respond by dry heaving.

Megan chuckled at it.

"Oh, come on. It's not that bad. It was a pretty clean snap. It was the last thing I heard, from what I can remember. Well, that, and the windshield breaking," Megan said.

"You're really dead! Holy shit!" Greg yelled.

"Yeah. It isn't so bad. This is a great spot in the summer. Watch the cars drive by, see some of the families play in their yards. Plus, Jeremy keeps me company. Did you meet him yet? He's such a sweet boy," Megan said.

"Is he the one with the big hole in the back of his head?" Greg asked.

Megan pointed at Greg in excitement. "That's him! Such a sweetheart. A little shy, though."

Greg picked up his bike and started pushing it up the hill. He paused for a second to contemplate his decision. *Was this a bad idea?*

Am I going to end up like Megan and Jeremy, wandering the side of this street like some sort of suburban limbo?

As nice as Megan was, it still creeped Greg out that he was talking to a dead girl with a disgusting injury that made him want to puke. He hadn't the first time, but if she showed him again, he knew puke was coming out after breathing so heavily from climbing the hill.

Greg looked toward the top, realizing he was more than halfway up. He needed to pass Western Avenue and finish the final stretch and try not to stop much since the remainder of the hill had deeper ditches that he definitely wasn't getting out of if he dropped again from exhaustion. He gave Megan a friendly wave.

"It was nice talking to you...Megan," Greg said. He forced a smile even though he was happier never seeing or talking to Megan again. He walked upward without waiting for her to respond.

"It was nice to meet you, too. Hey, be careful up there! Oh, make sure your helmet is buckled properly. Don't want the same thing that happened to Romon, happening to you," Megan said.

Greg froze. He didn't want to ask, but he was so curious as to why she didn't say what it was. He told himself to keep on walking, and he stepped forward to fight it, but he turned back to get more out of her. Especially about possibly meeting another dead person, and what the vague message would lead to.

When he looked where she'd been sitting, Megan was gone. Greg didn't want to try and try to find her and get a more horrible answer than what he'd already seen.

"You can do this. You can do this. Just keep going," Greg said to himself. "You can do-"

A blaring horn almost made Greg jump out of his skin. He looked back to see a white sports car driving past him quickly. "Get out of the road, dickhead."

"Fuck you, asshole," Greg said. He threw up his middle finger, nearly dropping his bike in the process. He gripped the handlebars firmly and pushed on. Then he saw someone in front of him. It was a hooded man standing off to the side of the road. Greg kept walking and tried not to look at him, even though he was going to walk right past him.

Was this who Megan warned me about? he thought.

"Don't sweat it, kid. This road got its name from the awful drivers," the hooded man said.

"Fuck. Fuck," Greg whispered to himself. He stopped and faced the man. "You're Romon, right?"

"Yeah. Megan told me about you. She's a sweet girl. Awful way to go for a girl like her," Romon said.

Romon stood tall, as he had the height advantage, and stood slightly higher on the hill. He avoided eye contact with Greg. It was easy to pull off since he had his hood up. He looked everywhere but directly at Greg when he spoke. He knew it was scaring Greg, because his hands shook slightly while he held his bike up.

Greg tried not to shake, but he felt so uneasy around Romon. "What... happened to you?" Greg asked.

"The same thing that happened to all of us. Hit by a car. Mine was a little different, though. Bad day to forget my helmet," Romon said as he pulled at the strings of his hoodie.

"Why have I never heard about any of these accidents? I only live ten minutes away from here," Greg said.

"We are from many different periods in time. I was hit nearly forty years ago. It's still kind of nice to see the neighborhood develop as it has. Wasn't this nice when I was growing up," Romon said.

Greg was a bit more at ease, knowing only a handful of people had died on this hill. No one in his thirteen years, as far as he knew, had

had a bad accident here, so what's the harm? Since these people were unfortunate in very particular incidents, he thought he should still continue on with his goal.

"Why was yours different?" Greg asked. He wanted to take back the question once the words left his lips.

"I don't know if you can handle it," Romon said.

"I can. I don't get squeamish easily. How bad can it be?" Greg asked.

"It makes Megan's look like a papercut," Romon said.

Greg didn't say anything. He'd wanted to puke out his huge breakfast as soon as he saw Megan tilt her head and fleshy insides poured out. He knew he'd actually puke if Romon had a drooping eyeball or exposed skull. He wanted to keep going up to the top of the hill, get on his bike, become a legend to all of his classmates, and put this whole experience behind him. Romon couldn't get in his head any further. He was already this far along.

"Try me," Greg said.

Romon looked at him for a second and nodded. Greg noticed something off in the brief nod, but let Romon continue. He pulled his hood back and revealed the rest of his head. The entire left side of his face was perfectly normal until he turned to reveal the right side, horrifying Greg immediately. If he did manage to become a legend from this ride, he would grow to an elderly man with this image burned into his head.

Romon's eye socket was a hollow black void, resting in his already dark complexion, that sat above a mass of torn flesh. The remaining teeth he had were all chipped and poking through his lip and cheek.

From his eyebrow to the top of his bald head was peeled back to expose parts of his brain, but mostly exposed skull. His ear was dangling on like a baby tooth that needed one quick pull to separate.

Greg wasn't sure, but it looked like Romon had tucked part of his cheek in so it wouldn't sway in the light breeze.

Greg had seen several horror films, some of which were more disgusting than others. He'd thought he could handle Romon's grotesque injuries when he'd first invited a view. Now, after seeing them, those horror movies he was so proud to have witnessed seemed like nothing but a waste of time. He dropped his bike, leaned forward, and shot vomit in front of Romon's feet. It poured out with ease, between the hill ascension and the sun having no clouds to dilute its intensity.

"Yeah, I figured your response would be something like that," Romon said as he pulled his hood back on. "Now you see what could happen when you don't listen to your parents about your helmet. In my case, I didn't listen to my wife. They always know."

"After today... I don't think I'll ride my bike at all. Goddamnit," Greg muttered, while expelling the last bit of chunks from his mouth. He reached to pull his bike up, barely able to lift it due to lack of strength from releasing so much from his gut. He let the bike stay on the ground.

After a brief glance, Greg saw some splashed vomit on the seat and back tire. The last thing he needed was his own bile and partly digested breakfast splattering all over him while descending rapidly down the hill. It needed some serious wiping before he took on the ride.

"Doom and Gloom is infamous to those who think they can handle one clear ride to the bottom. I don't think anyone has ever hit the bottom without a scratch," Romon said. "Do you really think it's worth your safety?"

"You did. So did Megan and that other boy. I just know I'm going to reach the bottom," Greg said. He didn't want Romon to mistake his confidence for arrogance. He had been planning this for weeks now and didn't want anything to stop him. "You have all given me little pieces to help my turn be safer and successful. I have my helmet. I know which parts to swerve at in case a car comes by too fast, and I know that the bottom is the difference between being some boring kid in school and being a legend until I graduate."

Romon had no response for a kid who thought he had the whole ride figured out. If exposed flesh and bone weren't an indicator that this kid should go home and play video games all day, then Greg was more foolish than Romon had first thought. He looked down at Greg, but he couldn't do a thing about it. So, he did what he thought was best, Romon stepped back, extended his arm, and pointed to the top of the hill.

"You have about thirty feet to go. Good luck, kid," Roman said. He smiled wickedly and turned to point his open socket at Greg. "See you at the bottom."

Greg quickly wiped off his bike with some leaves on the ground nearby and continued to climb up, pushing his bike with the remainder of the energy he had stored. Romon walked down the hill quickly.

Greg thought he was serious about standing at the bottom to watch, which was exciting to him. Whether Romon waited at the bottom of the hill or not, he was sure to see him one more time as he flew past on his bike.

Sweat poured heavily from Greg's forehead as he made the final ascent. He wanted to puke again and was regretting the lack of water he'd brought with him. He would drink an entire gallon once he was able to get to a nearby corner store, or hope that Brandon would bring some, knowing how hot the day was. He pushed with the little strength he had left and passed over the last hump that was Doom and Gloom.

Greg looked down, standing at the top of his first accomplishment. He dropped his bike and threw his arms in the air. He caught his breath and paced back and forth. He couldn't hold his smile in. Once he reached the bottom, he would be a legend. He stood at the top of Hudson Terrace, looking down the street and gazing at the view offered at the hilltop.

"Fuck all those kids who said I couldn't do this," Greg said. He took in a deep breath. "I am the king of Doom and Gloom!"

Just like the fellow inhabitants of the hill, another figure emerged in Greg's peripherals. A young boy sat across the street, crying, kneeling on the pavement. Greg walked over to see a young boy looking down at his cat. The cat was obviously dead, as a pool of blood formed around its nearly flattened midsection. The boy stared at Greg with tear-filled eyes.

"Can you help me? Someone ran over my cat," the boy cried.

"Hey, I'm sorry. Where are your parents?" Greg asked.

"I don't know. I can't find them. Please, my cat is hurt," he cried. "I don't want him to die."

Greg didn't have the heart to tell the boy the cat was already gone, but he wasn't going to let something happen to him since he was alone and vulnerable around cars.

"I don't know where you live. Can you show me?" Greg asked.

"I just want to play with him. He's my best friend," the boy cried. He leaned down to kiss his cat.

Greg couldn't look away from the gushing wound and the tire mark on the back of the boy's neck. He stared, mortified that he couldn't further decipher between these dead people and reality. He backed away and headed toward his bike. He hopped on, looking down the hill.

This was his defining moment to stand out, to defy the warnings the lingering lost souls warned him of, and to be infamous at his school. He put his foot on the pedal. He exhaled and let go of the ground as his other foot swung up to the second pedal. He was on his way down, fast.

Greg picked up speed quickly. He gripped the handlebars firmly, swaying down the path in a zig-zag to maintain a reasonable speed. Coming up to Western Avenue, he saw he was clear of any cars that may potentially ruin his mission. He sped past the stop sign and flew down the hill faster. He gained speed, more than he was comfortable with. He steadied in the small stretch of the flat street he rode down and then continued to pick up speed.

"Holy shit, I'm going to do it!" Greg yelled. He flew down the final stretch, hoping to catch Romon waiting at the bottom. To his surprise, he was right and saw Romon standing at the very bottom, looking up. Romon nodded in the distance, letting Greg know he was surprised he'd made it this far. Another thirty feet until his grand success.

"Go, Greg, go!" Megan yelled from the side of the road. Greg wanted to look over and give his approval of her support. He was too close to let himself crash and ruin his efforts, so he continued on. Twenty feet to go. The last bit of road was as clear as his visions of the fame and stardom he'd have when he reached the bottom.

Across the street, at the bottom of the hill, he saw Brandon waving at him and jumping up in the air. He needed at least one witness to confirm he actually did it, and Brandon came through as with that support. He had already planned to give Brandon some of his glory when the girls started talking to him more. Brandon was always a reliable friend, even if he was a bit of a pushover.

Ten feet to go. Greg gritted his teeth in excitement. The air was silent until he heard the blaring horn from behind him. He glanced over his shoulder to see the same white sports car from earlier was right at the back of his rear wheel. He looked back again to see himself touch the bottom of the hill.

Just seconds after, he felt himself fly over the handlebars. He was airborne, and the crunching sound of his bike being run over by the same asshole who'd startled him earlier was the last thing he heard. He put his arms in front of him before he touched the ground, and then his vision went black.

Greg opened his eyes. Megan hovered above him, and Romon glared at him from the other side of the street. Greg looked up to see his bike had bent forward, with no hope of repairing it.

"You did it. Someone finally did it!" Megan said. She hugged Greg. "You're a legend!" She walked away and made her way back up the hill.

Romon smiled at Greg. "I'll see you again soon, kid." He walked up the hill, fading as he ascended.

Greg lay flat as he composed himself from the heavy impact. He managed to swivel his head and look to his other side. He looked over at Brandon to see an expression of horror. He stared on, unable to speak. He dropped to his knees, spilling out all the bottled water he had ready for Greg.

"Brandon, what's-" Greg started, but stopped when he looked down at this body. His neck had turned completely around as he saw his back and butt. His elbows were pointing out, which immediately startled him. Brandon started crying and reached for his phone. He imagined he would call his mom to pick him up, or hopefully call an ambulance to pick up the remains of his friend.

Greg watched as Brandon walked further down the sidewalk, abandoning his bike, and finally sat down on the curb to cry and talk with whoever he was speaking to. He imagined Brandon was difficult to understand on the phone, as his face had become bright red and his eyes poured tears with more intensity than before.

Greg looked down at his body again, to see his legs facing behind him. He tried turning his neck slowly but found it difficult. With one big effort, his neck cracked loudly, and he was able to turn his head one hundred and eighty degrees with ease now. He sat up and pushed himself to his feet. He was as terrified as his distraught best friend was. He looked behind himself and grew more fearful when his neck kept turning beyond what it could a few hours ago. He stood, looking up Doom and Gloom, watching Megan and Romon ascend to their resting spots.

Greg knew he had died a legend, and would leave his legacy at that. It was up to Brandon to brag for him in school, when the time was right, after the grieving period. For now, Greg walked and stood at the base of the hill, where he properly belonged. He sat down and looked across at the mangled body he once knew, lying still.

He watched as first responders and a small crowd gathered to collect and investigate the scene. It felt like a matter of seconds for the entire experience. He watched them all go about their ways and he remained still, waiting to be another voice for the next thrill seeker.

4

While Sleeping

Alissa and her roommate, Matthew, sat on the couch watching television. Matthew changed the channel to find something for both of them to watch.

"Movie, ball game, show, or news?" Matthew asked.

"Let me think, Matthew. What do you think my answer will be?" Alissa asked.

"Good, the second quarter just started."

Alissa hit Matthew's arm. He kept flipping the channels and stumbled across a breaking news story.

"Two teenagers killed in a hit-and-run. No leads on the driver, or the whereabouts of their location. The victims' identities are unknown. We will have more as the story unfolds."

The news reporter covers minor details as Alissa sat up to listen carefully. Bodies were being wheeled away on stretchers, and enormous quantities of blood are were apparent in the background.

"Those poor people," Alissa said sadly.

"Maybe this isn't something we should watch before bed," Matthew said.

"Why?" Alissa asked.

"You told me you haven't been sleeping well," said Matthew. "I don't want you up all night thinking about it."

Alissa sat back into on the couch, turning off the television.

"I've just been having one weird recurring dream lately," Alissa said.

"What kind of dream?" Matthew asked.

Alissa leaned away from Matthew, resting against the arm of the couch.

"I don't want to talk about it," Alissa said. "It gives me the creeps, even after all this time."

Matthew moved closer to her, taking her hand. "It's just a dream. It won't hurt you."

Alissa took a deep breath. Matthew held her hand tightly. She looked at Matthew, who is watching her intently. She smiles.

"Okay, fine, here goes," Alissa said. "I have this dream where I'm lucid dreaming, and I'm in bed and can't sleep. Then I look over at the corner of the room, and this guy is just standing there."

"As in watching you sleep?" Matthew asked.

"Yes," Alissa said. "Just standing there, watching me. Then he leaves the room, and I sleep fine after that. The weird thing is that every night is the same thing, except last night."

"What happened last night?" asked Matthew.

"He looked at me, directly in the eye, and said 'Soon.'"

Matthew sat back and looked at her, strangely. He chuckled a little.

"What?" Alissa asked, irritated.

"Nothing. Just seems like nothing to worry about," Matthew said.

"Yeah, you're probably right. It's just a dream, as you say," Alissa said.

"That's right," said Matthew. "Now I'm going to bed."

"I want to watch some more T.V. for a little while. Have a good night," Alissa said.

"Okay. Goodnight," Matthew said.

Alissa smiled, and Matthew disappeared into the darkness. Alissa stared at the television, laughing at what was playing. Suddenly, an ominous figure emerged from the darkness of the hallway behind her. He walked up to the couch, staring down at her.

Alissa laughed at the television until it went to a commercial. The screen faded to black, and she sees a glimpse of someone standing behind her.

She slowly turned around to see a man with his arm stretched above his head, holding a knife. As she starts to scream, he wrapped his open hand around her head, covering her mouth.

SLASH!

He swung the knife down into her stomach and slid it out quickly. She grips her gut, applying pressure as she falls to the ground and crawls. She moved around the couch but sees the man step forward to cross her path. She slowly creeps beyond his foot and into the hallway.

"Matthew," Alissa whispered.

Blood poured from her stomach, leaving a small trail behind her. She looked back to see the man standing still.

"Matthew!" Alissa yelled. No answer came, and she dragged herself closer to the bedroom where Matthew slept. She looked back again in horror, to find the man stepping slightly closer to her.

The man's footsteps rattled Alissa's eardrums. Each step was like thunder inside their home. The already quiet home grew silent as the footsteps flooded the house. Alissa's eyes grew wide, as the drowning sound was all she could hear. She dug deep within herself to find the strength to get to Matthew. She crawled, she pulled toward the bedroom; she kicked her feet against the floor to push herself closer, inch by inch.

Then, when she was inches away from reaching the door frame, the crushing pressure of the man's foot stopped her leg. The heel of his foot shattered her ankle, making her stop right where she was. It was what Alissa was dreading, but it was what she needed to happen.

"MATTHEW!" Alissa screamed. The shriek of terror released the grip of her attacker. The sound of Matthew emerging from the bedroom gave her a moment of satisfaction.

Matthew came to the hallway to see Alissa bleeding and made eye contact with her attacker. The man charged Matthew, but Matthew charged back. The man swung his knife toward Matthew but was quickly blocked by Matthew's dominant strength. Matthew pinned the man against the wall, making him drop his knife.

"Who the fuck are you?" asked Matthew angrily.

"The one who will make things right," the man said.

Swiftly, the man pulled a blade from behind his back and drove it into Matthew's throat. Matthew stumbled back and fell to the floor while trying to pull the blade from his neck, but it was no use. The knife slid deeper as blood poured from the open wound. Blood drenched his shirt in seconds and soaked his pants as Matthew struggled to hold on. The man pushed hard, and the blade pierced him entirely up to the handle. Matthew goes limp as blood covers the rest of his clothing and then splatters to the floor. The man stands to look over at Alissa.

Alissa cries hysterically.

"No need to cry, Alissa," the man said. "This is a setback for the greater good."

"You... You know who I am?" Alissa asked.

The man smiled. He walked closer to Alissa and knelt next to her. He grabbed her by the throat. Alissa struggled to pull his hand from her neck, pushing and punching at him with little effect.

"It's why I'm here," the man said.

The man grips Alissa's throat tightly, picks her up, and slams her head into the floor, knocking her out. The man stands proudly as he looks back at the wreckage of blood and emotional trauma that will change this home ever forward. He drags Alissa toward the door.

"There is someone who wants to see you," the man said.

Alissa goes in and out of consciousness, awaiting her fate. The man drags her out into the night, as a second figure appears in front of car headlights.

"Is the roommate dealt with?" the second figure asked. "I can't have anyone ruining this for me."

"Yes, Doctor. Shall I bring her to her room now?" the man asked.

"Please. I look forward to seeing how long she will last in her recurring dream," the doctor said. He knelt in front of Alissa, locking eyes with her as she faded in and out of consciousness.

Alissa looked at the doctor as a smile spread across his face. She stared at him until the light faded from her vision and the trunk door closes above her.

5

Orb

Alan emerged from unconsciousness. His first movements reveal excruciating pain all over his body. He looked down to find himself covered in bruises, deeply cut all over his face and chest, and soaked in blood. He attempted to stand and cried out in pain.

Several bullet holes in his pants let him know why his legs won't support the rest of his body. Unable to move his legs, he crawled. He tumbled down a hill and landed on a mysterious black orb, full of spots of color, and examined it.

"Where did you come from?" Alan asked, gazing into the orb. He found himself unable to turn away, as if it hypnotized him. Alan couldn't blink and could barely breathe. A powerful ringing engulfed his hearing, causing him intense pain.

He dropped the orb and took a deep breath. His vision was blurry as the orb overpowered him and put him in a trance. A girl appeared before him.

"Hello," she said.

"Who are you?" Alan asked. "Where did you come from?"

"I can help you," she said. "I can help you seek vengeance."

"Vengeance?" Alan asked. "Vengeance from who?"

Alan froze. He couldn't bring himself to get any closer to her since he was wounded for reasons that were still a mystery. She pointed at Alan. He was a little thrown off until he realized that his wounds related to her statement of getting vengeance. He examined the wounds thoroughly. There was no logic behind him surviving such gruesome injuries.

"The men who gave you those," the girl said.

"Who are you?" Alan asked.

"Madeline," she said.

Madeline walked closer to Alan and placed her hand on his back. She looked down at him and smiled.

"You will need your strength," Madeline said. In an instant, Alan felt a surge of energy fill his body. She healed his wounds and mangled legs enough for him to stand.

Alan climbed to his feet and examined his body, finding no injuries.

"Where did you come from, Madeline?" Alan asked with intense confusion.

Madeline pointed down to the orb. "You set me free," Madeline said.

Alan grew skeptical of the reality of the current situation. He felt light-headed from his physical pain. He took a step toward her and reached to touch her. She stood perfectly still as Alan's hand passed through her, like an apparition.

"This is in my head," Alan said with skepticism. "You aren't real."

Alan walked away from her. He turned back to see she had vanished completely. He grabbed the orb and walked into the distance until he reached the end of the tree-line. He approached a nearby park in search of aid to reach home.

SEVERAL WEEKS WENT BY after the incident in the woods. Alan always questioned the events that transpired that evening. Was he drugged? Did he take hallucinogens and forget? It was all too peculiar to him, as his friends only remember him leaving their house that night and resurfacing the next night. It was a shock to Alan that someone had left him for dead, and not a single soul knew about it.

Alan suddenly felt an odd presence in his apartment. After looking through every room, he opened the door to see only the hallway wall on the other side. Peering down the hallway made him more confused, as no one was around nor even making noise. He closed the door and turned back into his living room. He jumped back when he noticed Madeline standing in front of him.

"Jesus Christ, what is this?" Alan questioned.

"You still have yet to find those responsible for your attack," Madeline said.

"I don't want to. I want to forget it ever happened. Just leave me alone." Alan sat on the couch and flipped through the channels on the television.

Madeline approached him and stood over him, looking down. She placed her hand on his shoulder.

"Do you not remember what they did to you?" Madeline asked.

"No, and I don't think I want to," Alan said.

"It is necessary for you to see it again," Madeline said. She gripped both sides of Alan's head and squeezed with all of her strength. Alan's body became paralyzed. His vision went blank, as his only sight was a bright white light. He sees the moment he was in the woods.

A DISTANT GUNSHOT ECHOED into the forest as stray pellets from a shotgun blast ripped into Alan's legs. He dropped to the ground. One hunter ran up to him. Alan gripped his legs in agony as the hunter stood over him. A second hunter reached them, and they both looked down at Alan.

"See, Keith, I told you it wouldn't kill him from that distance," Benny said, chuckling.

"So, finish it here, dumbass," Keith said, handing the shotgun to Benny.

Benny cocked another shell into the chamber. Alan swung his fist into Benny's groin, making him drop the shotgun. Benny clutched himself and yelled out in agony.

"You piece of shit!" Keith exclaimed as he swung his boot into Alan's gut.

Alan let out a loud groan. He sat on Alan's chest and hit him in the face. He swung over and over until Alan stopped moving. Alan looked up into the sky out of his right eye. His left eye, swollen shut and bloodied, remained closed to Keith standing above him, catching his breath.

"Come on, Benny, finish it." Keith picked up the shotgun and passed it to Benny. He points it toward Alan's head.

BANG!

Gunshots echoed nearby. Benny and Keith ducked, looking in all directions.

"Goddamn city guys can't fucking handle themselves. Let this asshole bleed out. Come on," Keith said.

Keith and Benny ran off into the woods. Through the blurred vision that Alan had left, he watched them disappear over the hill. He returned his gaze toward the sky and listened to the calming sounds while the gunshots momentarily ceased. He heard footsteps approaching.

Have they come to finish me for good? Is this someone that could help me? Alan pondered.

"Fucker ran off, and you got the shot. Just my luck."

"I told you I'd get a buck before you. Better luck next time, Jerry."

Two voices came and went by. Alan peered over to the right and saw camouflage suits gradually walk off into the woods. Alan tried to get words out, but his swollen face wouldn't allow him the volume needed to save himself from lying there in agony.

Please, come back. Don't let me die here, he thought.

He tried getting to his feet, but the pain radiated to his waist. He knew the bulk of the shot went into his thigh, but only noticed when he tried to stand that a stray pellet had pierced his gut. A small bit of blood soaked through his shirt.

I have to move. It's the only way I'll make it.

Alan crawled. He didn't know what direction he was going in, so he just moved. He crawled, and he crawled. The pain was mild as long as he put most of his weight on his good leg. He reached to pull himself further, but came to the edge of a steep hill. He tumbled down on all of his wounds. He cried out each time his broken body struck a rock or mound of dirt.

After landing, he caught his breath and positioned himself so he could tolerate the pain he'd just endured, on top of the wounds that were reaching a critical level. That's when he spotted it. An orb. He looked at it for several seconds before crawling toward it.

As Alan's eyes focused on the orb, his vision blurred and stretched deep into tunnel vision. Alan snapped back to the present.

MADELINE STOOD IN THE center of the room, glaring at him. They locked eyes.

"Those men don't deserve to get away with what they did to you. Do you disagree?" Madeline asked.

Alan knew she was right. He barely remembered the incident, but with Madeline's help, he could punish them for their actions.

"Can you get me to them?" Alan asked.

"I can. Take this. It will show you the way." Madeline handed the orb to Alan. He glanced down at it and looked up to notice she had vanished.

The orb glowed dimly. Alan grabbed his jacket and headed for the door. He got to his car, starting it. The orb glowed brightly, and Alan suddenly knew the route to find the men who had tried to kill him. Madeline didn't speak to him at all.

Once the orb glowed this time, it was as if the route was a distant memory, recently resurfaced. Alan drove into the night, with the view of their cabin plain as day in his mind.

Alan turned off of the highway and drove deeper into the woods. Even the high beams were inferior to the darkness that swallowed the immediate area. Further down the road, he saw lights shining from the windows of a small cabin. He turned off his high beams and drove slowly toward his uncertain fate. The orb glowed brighter than ever before. Alan covered part of his face to shield himself from the light he was sure would blind him.

The orb spoke, "It is here."

"This is their place?" Alan asked.

"They are inside—the ones who tried to take your life."

Alan turned off the headlights. He slowed to a stop and turned off the engine. The orb's brightness faded as the engine quieted to a soft hum before stopping completely. He opened the car door slowly, hoping they wouldn't hear him.

"Approach slowly. You will have a chance if you remain quiet."

Alan crept toward the front door slowly. He heard the voices of two men from the slightly ajar door.

"Here's to another poor sap who won't see his family again," Benny said, clanking his beer against Keith's.

"Think we can get one more tomorrow?" Keith asked, smiling widely.

"One? I'm going for two myself," Benny said. "Then we move on to another spot, Benny?" Keith asked.

"Before they can find us, we will settle in new hunting grounds," Benny said.

"Sounds like a brilliant plan," Keith said.

Alan walked toward their pickup truck for cover and peered into the open bed. A dead deer was draped in a large tarp that dangled toward the ground. Beneath the tarp, a black handle stuck out. Alan slid it out, revealing the rest of the shotgun body.

One voice had gotten louder. Alan knelt behind the pickup truck and was able to see into the living room where they sat. The silence of the night radiated into the trees, making it easy for Alan to hear the two inside.

"Forgot something in the truck, Benny. I'll be right back," Keith said.

The door opened wide, and Keith walked into the front yard. He peered up at the sky for a moment.

"Now's your chance."

Alan looked down at the shotgun. He swung it straight out in front of himself. He stood up and took aim at Keith, cocking a shell into the chamber. Keith changed his upward gaze and looked over at Alan. His hands raised above his head as he stood perfectly still.

"Easy now," Keith whispered. "No need for any of that."

"I think there's plenty of need for this, after what you did to me." Alan took a step forward and stopped when Keith's eyes widened. He had realized who Alan was, and all the fear he felt inside erupted on his face in a blatant expression.

"Do it now."

"BENNY!" Keith yelled. "COME QUICK, BENNY!"

BANG!

The shotgun blast echoed through the trees, and Keith went flying across the yard as the many pellets ripped through his skin and took his balance away. He landed on his neck, and his body slammed to the ground shortly after.

Several of the pellets had exited his body, but many were still lodged in his face, making it apparent to Alan the single shot he'd taken was enough. He stepped over the pool of blood that formed around Keith and walked toward the door.

"Finish the last one."

Alan kicked the door in, swinging it hard against the wall. Benny shot to his feet from his reclining chair.

"Who the fuck are you?" Benny asked in shock and frustration at being startled out of his seat.

"You left me to die in the woods when you and your dead friend shot me," Alan scolded. "Now, on your knees. I wasn't hesitant with your friend."

"Lucky for me, you weren't," Benny chuckled.

"What does that mean?" Alan asked.

"It means that I fired that gun last before you picked it up. There was only one shot left." Benny stepped closer to Alan.

Alan squeezed the trigger and heard nothing but more silence that haunted his next several moments. He locked eyes with Benny, who was slowly drawing a knife from the sheath attached to his belt. Alan swung the shotgun into Benny's arm, launching the knife across the room.

"Motherfucker!" Benny swung his leg directly into Alan's gut.

Alan dropped to the ground, but barely had enough time to clench his throbbing abdomen before Benny sat on top of him. Benny swung his fists into Alan's face, and each hit became bloodier than the last. Alan's eye puffed up, while his lip looked as if he'd applied lip balm with razor blades. His vision blurred, as one eye was now useless. His only thoughts in the fading consciousness were how he needed to get Benny off of him.

His hand wandered around the nearby floor. He felt the butt of the shotgun. As two more punches nearly fractured his eye socket, he gripped the gun and swung it toward Benny. The gun aligned with Benny's temple, knocking him to the ground and forcing his eyes to stray in all directions.

"You fucker. Damn, that hurt." Benny looked around, dazed. Blood dripped from the ear that hit the ground. His temple grew to a shade of red from the impact.

Alan rolled over to onto his stomach. He spat out blood while rising to his feet. He pulled the shotgun up with him, bracing himself on it for support while he wiped his face. He swung the gun down across Benny's back with all his strength. Benny wailed out in pain.

"I'll kill you right this time. No mistaking it!" Benny lunged for Alan's feet until he felt another hard swing across his back. He cried out in agony. "Fuck you, I'll soak this floor with your blood!"

Alan didn't hesitate to swing the gun across Benny's face, splattering blood across the room as Benny's nose, lips, and teeth crunched from the impact with the butt of the shotgun. Benny was silent while he held onto his face with both hands. Alan knew he'd done serious damage when the spaces between Benny's fingers flowed red.

Alan searched for shells for the shotgun. He spotted a box on a shelf and loaded two into the barrel. He kicked Benny onto his back and pushed his arms away from his face. Benny was hardly recognizable as his missing teeth, swollen eye, and disfigured, broken nose change the appearance of the man Alan had walked in to see tonight. Alan cocked the gun, sticking it right against Benny's forehead.

"Can you feel the power they felt?"

Alan froze, listening to Madeline. The rest of the world went silent while Madeline spoke to Alan.

"Take his life as they planned on doing to you."

"You... don't have it in you," Benny muttered from his mangled face. "You ain't no killer."

BANG!

The shotgun erupted into Benny's face, and his head sprayed across the floor. Skull and brains went under the nearby couch, while blood scattered like paint drops across the walls and floor. The bridge of Benny's nose was the highest remaining point of his head. His arms lay still on the ground. Alan, now drained of his residual energy, dropped the gun and sat on the floor.

"You did it. You avenged me."

Madeline appeared behind Alan. He stood abruptly, stunned by her manifestation.

"Avenged you? What are you talking about?" Alan asked.

"I was taking a walk in the woods behind my house one afternoon. My mother gave me a beautiful gift for my birthday. It was so black, but the colors glowed like the night sky. I couldn't put it down. I didn't want to look at anything else all day. I wanted to be at peace with my beautiful gift. He grabbed me so fast that I didn't even notice my pants were off until he forced himself on me. Even while enduring the entire experience, all I wanted to do was get lost in the colors. It was the last thing I saw before he took my life. The next thing I knew, I was inside of it. It wasn't until you touched it that I could escape. You set me free."

Madeline handed Alan the orb. He stared into it, lost in her words.

"I'm sorry that happened to you," Alan said.

"It's okay, Alan. I learned to accept it. I want it to be a message to you, and to the next person who needs my power. It's important we remember that our anger needs to escape. These two didn't deserve to live anymore. The punishment appropriate for their wrongdoings happened tonight. I'm not a victim anymore, but I'm a message for anyone else who forgets the darkness in their heart."

Alan looked up at Madeline and then back down at the orb. He placed the orb on the shelf next to her.

"The darkness in my heart left, Madeline," Alan said. "I don't need this anymore."

Alan walked toward the door, stepping over the masses of flesh and blood he'd left scattered on the floor. He looked back at Madeline one last time.

"Goodbye, Alan," Madeline said.

Alan walked out of the cabin and headed toward his barely visible car. He drove off into the night. The cabin and Madeline disappeared into the darkness.

SEVERAL DAYS PASSED AFTER Alan's encounter at the cabin. A large jeep approached the cabin. The passenger door swung open as soon as the engine shut off and Howard jumped out onto the driveway. Justin stepped out of the driver's seat and closed his door softly. He looked over at the pickup truck and then to the front door that's cracked open.

"My money says they're still drunk and lost their phones," Howard said.

"You don't have any money. I always pay," Justin said. "You get what I mean, asshole," Howard scolded.

Justin walked toward the house. He looked into the bed of the truck to see the deer under the tarp swarmed by flies. He covered his face once the smell hit his nose.

"Howard, did you teach your boy to-"

Justin saw Keith from the other side of the truck. He noticed Keith had died some timesometime in the last two days. His face, pale as snow, stared into the sky.

The shredded shirt and blood drained every bit of movement from Justin's legs.

"Keith!" Justin ran toward his mangled son. He examined the many wounds across Keith's chest and lower face. Justin looked over at Howard. "Benny can't be far."

"Benny! Hey! Benny!" Howard shouted as he rushed into the cabin. A moment of silence haunted Justin as Howard stormed the cabin and saw Benny all over the floor and walls.

"Oh, God! Benny! My boy!" It was the only answer they both knew was coming.

Justin rushed into the cabin to see the horror of yet another mangled son. The shotgun Alan had left was only feet away from Benny's body. Howard reached for it, but Justin stopped him.

"Don't. Wait for the cops," Justin said.

"No cop or sheriff can stop what I'll do to the cock sucker who did this to our boys. I'll gut him right in front of his parents!" Howard shouted.

"Something in here has to tell us what happened," Justin said. "I'll look around."

Justin wandered and examined the room slowly. Howard fought tears for as long as possible, but he gave in when he looked at the dog tags around Benny's neck that Howard gave him when he was a child. Benny loved the tags just as much as Howard.

Justin approached a shelf, spotting a black orb with vast colors inside. He picked it up and stared into it. His eyes glowed from the reflection of the orb taking in the light coming from the open door. The orb briefly blinded Justin, and he dropped it back on to the shelf.

"Holy shit," Justin said. "Hey, is this Benny's? I've never seen Keith with something like this."

"What is it?" Howard asked.

"Some kind of ball. I think it's glass." Justin handed the orb to Howard. He inspected it, thoroughly, but felt confused by what he was admiring.

"It's powerful, you know," Madeline said, emerging from behind Justin. Howard shot back, startled by Madeline's sudden presence, dropping the orb back on the shelf. Justin took a few steps back. Madeline stood still.

"Where the fuck did you come from?" Howard asked.

"The orb. It's where I stay until I'm needed," Madeline said.

"Who are you?" Justin asked.

"A victim, like your sons," Madeline said. "I connect with the victims for that very reason. I'm here to aid you both."

"Do you know who did this?" Howard asked.

"I do. I can bring you to him. I am the vengeance you crave. Let my powers help you both," Madeline said. She pointed toward her orb. "Use my power to get justice for your sons."

Justin reached for the orb and looked at it before handing it to Howard. Madeline walked out the front door, followed closely by Howard and Justin.

6

Pet

"You will be late for school again!" Alex's mother shrieked.

Alex jumped out of bed. He got dressed in a panic. Another late, agonizing night that disrupted the ebb and flow of his somewhat regular schedule. He stood to see Fang, drooling, chewing on his now-destroyed sneaker.

"Goddamnit, Fang!" Alex yelled. He pulled the shoe from his aggressive dog's grasp, and he growled at Alex.

"Yeah, yeah, a tough guy as always," he said to his four-legged opponent. Alex went into his closet and pulled out a replacement shoe from the pile of mismatched sneakers Fang hadn't destroyed. Sure, he could take the ridicule from kids at school again. Alex wished he didn't have to buy new sneakers every week.

Alex ran downstairs and inhaled his food. His mom was glaring at the news, like every morning.

"Another attack on a local dog. The dog, mutilated, laid on the front porch of the family home," the reporter says.

"We loved Willy. He was such a sweet dog toward the kids and us. Whatever wild animal did this must either be captured or put down immediately.

There is no need for another family to suffer like we have," Jake Ross, the dog's owner, says to the news reporter.

"You better lock Fang up today. I won't be responsible for him," Alex's mom said.

Alex rolled his eyes and continued eating. His mom always lacked any belief he could take care of Fang, which he had done for four years. The school bus rolled up, and Alex ran toward the door. Another morning, he'd barely stay awake, even with the extra caffeine intake at school.

Alex got home late after studying with Kevin to find Fang in his room.

"Hey buddy, sorry I got home so late," Alex said to him. That's when he noticed it. Fang had something all over his mouth. Alex walked closer and realized his worst fear–coated dry blood.

"Fang, what did you do?" Alex asked. Fang sat down and barked at him. He walked closer and stood over his pet to assert authority.

"Fang!" Alex yelled. He jumped and ran to the door, then down the hallway.

Alex ran after him. He chased Fang through the kitchen, out the back door, and into the backyard. He stopped by the tree in the corner of the yard. Alex saw something else, and the breath in his lungs vanished.

A whimper echoed into in Alex's ear and down into his sinking stomach as he saw the eviscerated dog drag itself closer. He fell back, helpless, as he noticed its back legs were completely severed. Alex looked over at Fang in anger. He reached for Fang, but before he could grab him, Fang growled at Alex. The growl evolved into a snarl as Alex stared back into his eyes.

"Fang, no," Alex scolded.

Fang grew angrier, snarling loudly. Drool poured from his mouth, and his teeth grew more visible with every breath he took.

"Fang, stop it!" Alex yelled.

Then, right on cue, like last night, Fang changed. His jaw expanded wider, and his tongue curled back into his throat like a rolled carpet. His eyes flipped back into his head, and darkness filled the whites of his eyes, like the noon sky drastically transitioning to midnight. His entire face folded back and presented a whole additional set of teeth that appeared to hide in his skull.

Alex had to admit, even though he had seen this happen twenty or thirty times by now, it still terrified him. When he finished, and his face was almost entirely teeth, Fang let out a shriek that was terrifying enough to make the already dying dog whimper until it rested its head one final time. Alex let out a sigh and gently put his hand on the deceased dog's head.

"I'm sorry," Alex whispered, "'I'm doing my best to control him."

Alex stared down at Fang as he returned to his usual dog self. He went to get the shovel from the side of the house, grabbed a black bag, and shoveled the carcass inside. This would be another body for Alex to move elsewhere. If he tried to bury another dog in this yard, his parents would surely notice. He tied the bag up and pulled it over his shoulder.

"Come on, boy, let's go," Alex chided, as if he were a disappointed father finding something his child shouldn't have. They walked into the night and into the woods.

Alex packed the dirt down and let the shovel rest against a tree. He took a deep breath, winded from the digging, lifting, and packing. He peered over at Fang, who now seemed relaxed, like a cranky child after their tantrum. He made eye contact with Alex and whimpered. Fang ran up to his leg and cuddled close.

"Fang, I can't be doing this forever. Someone will eventually find out. That means either they take you away, they kill you, or they get much bigger dogs to challenge you," Alex said.

Fang barked with excitement. Almost as if the last option enticed him. Still, even the most violent pet's pet owner has a soft spot for their pet. Alex wasn't different from them. He's buried more dead dogs than his whole neighborhood combined.

It's amusing how Alex can forgive Fang every single day, even after he's making Alex out to be a suspect for local pet murders. Still, Alex knew no one could handle what kind of dog Fang truly was. Fang is an exceptional pet, overall.

7

Gone, Mother

Seth reaches for his phone and dials his mother.

The call goes to a recorded voicemail message. His mother's voice is soothing at the other end. The beep alerts him to say what he isn't able to say to her directly.

"Mom, it's Seth. I wanted to thank you for the sweater and gloves. They look great on me. Your knitting is better than that shit I pay too much for at the store. These will be wonderful when it gets colder. I'll call you tomorrow and we can talk about vacation arrangements. I love you."

Seth hangs up the phone. He puts his sweater and gloves on the hanger. He enters the kitchen and approaches the refrigerator. He pulls down a note under a magnet labeled "Mom's Recipe". He reads through it and places it on the counter in front of several baking pans.

"Okay, let's do this," Seth says to himself.

Three Days Later

Seth picks up his phone and dials his mother. He reaches her voicemail again.

"Mom, it's Seth again. I must have missed you. Just calling to see how you are. I really appreciate you calling me for my birthday yesterday. I wish I could've answered your call. Anyway, I love you. I will try calling you later tonight."

Two Days Later

Seth calls his mother while cooking dinner.

"Mom, it's me. I'm calling to let you know I'm using your recipe for a house party this weekend. Some of my friends tried it the other day and insisted I bring it over. Thank you for giving me this. I really appreciate you helping me out. I'm happy to see so many other people admire your food as much as I do. Anyway, call me back when you get a chance. I love you."

Seth hangs up and places his food in a pan. He lets it cool on the stove while cleaning up the kitchen.

Five Days Later

Seth dials his mother's number. He once again reaches her voicemail.

"Mom, it's Seth again. I hope you are doing well. I was wondering if you checked the mail lately. I sent you something a few days ago.

I know you tell me you don't need material things, but I saw it and couldn't resist getting it for you. It's something to show you how much I love you. Please call me back when you get it, okay? I'll talk to you soon. I love you."

Seth hangs up and walks toward his bedroom.

Four Days Later

Seth stops to look at the calendar. He locks on today as if he sees a ghost emerging from the wall to reach out and grab him. It was a date marked "One Year". Seth, looking down at the floor, calmly walks into his bedroom. He emerges with his coat and exits his home.

THE SUN HAD DISAPPEARED into the horizon hours before. Streetlights and headlights were the only sources lighting Seth's journey home. He stumbled when he opened his apartment door and fell onto the floor, hard. Sounds of objects crashing to the floor echo in his ear.

His inebriated brain struggles to acknowledge his broken possessions and how he got to the ground so quickly. He struggles to pull his cell phone from his pocket. He dials his mother. The voicemail answers instead of his mother's voice.

"Mom, it's your son. I want to apologize. I've called you more times this week than I have in the last two years. I know that doesn't make up for anything at all, but I want to take it all back. I wish I could talk to you again, instead of having hopes of you answering. I want more time with you, instead of my grief for you. Not telling you how much you meant to me before you passed will haunt me for the rest of my life. There is no sentiment in talking to empty rooms, but I love you and I always will love you. Goodbye, Mom."

Seth drops the phone, sobbing intensely. In the next room, lying on the floor, is a broken picture frame. Broken glass pierced a photo of Seth and his mother.

8

THE LAST TIME I SAW YOU

SAM HAD THE HOUSE to himself. His wife had left with the kids for the afternoon, to get them stuffed with cake and junk food at a birthday party. Sam finally sat down at his computer to finish working after a tedious session of chores. The dishes were clean, he'd done the laundry, and he had a takeout menu to get himself through a lonely Saturday night.

The doorbell rang, and Sam walked to get it. It was irritating, as he had just gotten comfortable. Sam pulled the door open to see a glare reflect off the face of someone he should recognize. The glass door between Sam and the familiar face blinded them momentarily from seeing one another until the person stepped forward.

"It has been a very long time. I hope you remember me," he said.

The glass door swung open and Sam's estranged Uncle Matt stood there as if they had seen each other recently. Sam took a step back out of confusion and intense frustration. He hadn't heard from his uncle for almost fifteen years. It shocked Sam that his uncle had found where he lived.

"How... how are you?" Sam asked. Uncle Matt smiled and reached in for some physical contact. Sam backed up slightly, as he wasn't sure if he was living in reality at the moment. Sam felt bad about the withdrawal, but he knew the entire moment was weird, even for his uncle.

"I'm doing well. It's good to see you," Uncle Matt said.

Sam's mind was racing toward a reason for his presence here. Did he need money? Were my parents aware of his abrupt visit to my house? Was he in trouble of some kind? After a while, Sam felt his uncle notice his confusion, as it most likely overcame his expression, like paint splatter on a blank canvas.

"I know it may be weird I-" Uncle Matt started. "Why exactly are you here, after all these years?"

Sam asked sternly. It suddenly occurred to Sam that this man had answered none of the family's means of communication for as long as he could remember. The entire family had become baffled by years of absence. They worried about who this man had become, and feared who he might not be anymore.

"Can I come in to talk?" Uncle Matt asked.

Sam didn't know how to answer that question. After all this time, he was still angry at his uncle for not reaching out to the family in any regard. Part of him wanted to forgive everything. No amount of anger would fix this, but it still burned inside, especially since Uncle Matt turned up unannounced.

"I don't think I'm okay with that," Sam said. Uncle Matt worked up a smile and stepped forward.

"Please. I think it will benefit us both," Uncle Matt said, stepping past Sam in the doorway. Now Sam couldn't help but face him and what he did. He closed the door behind himself and walked into the living room where his uncle had already helped himself to a seat.

"Anything to drink?" Sam asked, even though he was reluctant to even speak to his uncle.

"No, thank you," Uncle Matt said. Sam sat beside him, and the moment felt heavy. Sam felt as if he needed to break the tension. His uncle stared at him, smiling patiently, as if he were waiting for Sam to be the first to speak.

"So, why exactly are you here now?" Sam asked.

Sam could tell there was composure in him, which Sam struggled to have at the moment.

"It's obvious that we've had little of a relationship since you were a child," Uncle Matt said.

"I'd argue none," Sam scolded. Uncle Matt maintained his smile with his composed body language.

"Your parents or your sister never had the emotional strength you had growing up. There was always something that kept you a little tougher than them. Maybe because you were a boy, or you weren't aware of everything, but I always admired that. I knew that if the day came to face all of you, I should start with you," Uncle Matt said.

Sam didn't know how to respond to that. He hoped his uncle kept speaking so he could make sense of all of this.

"My life has challenged my will more than I can ever explain to you. I've spent years understanding what, exactly, I can do to help my situation improve. In doing so, I've distanced the most important people who should be right by my side. Our family was always the missing piece that I could never see in the entire picture. You guys are everything I needed," Uncle Matt said.

The light in his smile faded toward sorrow. Tears filled his eyes, and Sam tried his best to hold it together. Uncle Matt wiped his eyes before he kept speaking. "It may be too late, but I am sorry. I took too long to realize what was right in front of me," Uncle Matt said. "If it is any consolation, my life has only gotten better since I gained the courage to knock on your door."

After Uncle Matt finished, he let out a deep exhale. Sam could feel the tension release from his body. His slight slouch gave Sam the sign that this had been growing inside of him for quite some time. Sam was no longer angry with him. He finally felt the relief that he'd wanted for so long.

"I know that was hard to say. I appreciate it," Sam said, smiling at his uncle. He smiled back, and that helped both of them ease the tension they'd had when sitting down. "When do you plan on seeing Mom and Dad?"

"When the time is right. For now, I'm just happy that we could reconcile after so many years. I am finally at peace with it," Uncle Matt said. The tension had diminished from his body language. He even seemed like it tired him.

"Can I get you anything? You look pretty tired," Sam said. Uncle Matt looked down at the floor and then made eye contact with Sam.

"I'm okay. I need to step outside for a moment," Uncle Matt said, rising to his feet. Sam stood and walked him toward the door. Uncle Matt looked back at Sam with urgency, gripping his shoulder. He wasn't just looking into his nephew's eyes, he was looking into his mind.

"Thank you for giving me a chance. It means everything to me," Uncle Matt said. Sam could tell there was urgency behind it. Almost like it would be a long time before they would see each other again. Sam struggled to find words, as the look was so piercing.

"You... you got it," Sam said.

"If you don't mind, I'll take a glass of water from you," Uncle Matt said in a soft voice.

"Sure thing," Sam said. Uncle Matt let his grip loosen as Sam turned to enter the kitchen. He grabbed a glass, ran it under the faucet, and made his way back into the hallway.

"Here you-," Sam tried to say. Uncle Matt had vanished as if he were never there. Sam didn't see him outside, or in any of the rooms.

"Hello?" Sam called out, hearing no answer. The house echoed with the silence that he recalled before this bizarre encounter. It made no sense to him.

Was it all in my head? Why now? Why here?

Sam's phone vibrated in his pocket. He pulled it out, saw it was his mom, and answered.

"Hey, Mom. How are you?" Sam asked.

"Son, I have something to tell you about your uncle," she said.

Somehow, Sam already knew what she would say. He felt it immediately. This entire encounter over the last twenty minutes had had an unusual feeling about it. It was a surreal moment that Sam couldn't compare to anything he'd experienced before. Sam knew when he'd turned the corner to find his uncle gone, that it wasn't normal—it was a fleeting moment that would stick with him forever.

"This will be difficult to tell you. You should sit down for this," she said.

Little did she know that Sam already knew. Whether his experience was real or something else entirely, he knew this was something that would only happen for him. Regardless, he'd made his peace with it, and his late uncle.

9

I Love This City

Four o'clock on the dot and Holly flew out of her seat. Monday prep can wait this time around, she thought. Typically, she sorted paperwork so her next week could be better, but today Holly didn't care one bit. She grabbed her bag, threw on her coat to brace the winter fury, headed for the elevator, and descended as quickly as she could. The door opened, and Holly peered at the people scurrying like bugs upon at the sight of extermination. She joined them to make it to the nearest subway station.

The platform quickly filled with commuters awaiting the next train to take them away into the night, and home from the tiring week. As she ventured into the beautiful yet ominous city, Holly stared at many of them, wondering what others do to suspend the torment of the week. The train car opened, and Holly sat in a full seat.

Each stop simultaneously collected and delivered the white collars and vagabonds to their destinations. The train car slowly got darker as the sun retreated for nighttime's reign. The train grew emptier as the last stop left only an older gentleman and Holly at the station, who peered over at her with suspicion.

"Young lady, what on earth brings you so far into this neighborhood at this hour?" he asked. Holly had to admit; this was the first time she'd gotten down here so early. However, she had an interminable night ahead of her. Holly needed to do quite a few things before Saturday showed its presence in her schedule.

"I have a friend who lives nearby. He wanted to show me his new apartment," Holly said.

"Well, please be safe. Some people have different manners in this part of town," he said in a stern tone. Holly couldn't help but smile.

"I will," she said.

She pushed forward and walked the two blocks without so much as an aggressive catcall and only two whistles. The apartment had a steel door and a blue wooden door behind it that appeared to have deep slashes from some vicious animal. The doorbell was piercing and loud. The door swung open.

"Holly, the Queen of Night!" Rodney yelled.

She chuckled when Rodney approached her after clearing his makeshift home security. He hugged her tight. Way too tight. He was a behemoth, towering almost seven feet tall. Muscular, with tattoos that would make an inmate cringe, while smiling wide with four missing teeth. His tattooed bald head, riddled with the quality of a child's drawing, was just the icing on the cake.

"Get in here. I have what you asked for," Rodney said.

They climbed the stairs to his master bedroom. Many locks decorated the battered door. He stopped before opening it to show her the wonders he had inside.

"I'm thrilled you could make it out here tonight. Today is a special day. I brought two things you asked me for," Rodney said.

"You never let me down, Rodney," Holly said, smiling.

"Still no luck on taking you out, though, right?" Rodney asked with enthusiasm glowing from his hideous smile.

"You know you couldn't handle me," Holly said kindly.

"Yeah, you would kill me. At least you still keep me around, though. Come on," he said.

After several moments of watching Rodney toy with the locks, Holly peered into the bedroom. A bare mattress, with a tattered pillow, lay in the room's center. Rodney had lined up six men by the wall.

All of them had hoods over their heads, to cover their muffled screams and to conceal their current location. On the wall was an assortment of firearms that Rodney had retrieved from these same men. They were mounted like decorative art pieces in an expensive gallery.

"Your firearms, and the men you asked for," Rodney said, bowing to present them to Holly with chivalrous grace. They moved closer, and Holly examined the weapons on the wall.

"I would've gotten you the rest of the men, but I killed two. I have their bodies in the basement freezer. I hope you can forgive me for this. Please accept a pass on my payment this week as my sincere apology," Rodney said.

Holly picked up an Uzi. She examined it and cocked it. She sprayed one of the hooded men, killing him instantly, and watched as his stiff corpse slammed onto the floor. The rest of the men screamed beneath their duct-taped mouths and hoods.

"These are the men who should face my wrath. Not you, my dear," Holly said as she cocked back a pump-action shotgun. She fired it into another man, throwing him against the wall, showering bone fragments and blood from his body.

"I think I heard his neck break from that one," Rodney said, chuckling.

"Please look at this one. The trigger sticks." Holly shows Rodney the shotgun, nodding and gently placing it on his mattress. Holly picks up a revolver and loads three rounds into the chamber. She spins the cylinder and walks over to the next man.

"Why only three rounds, Holly?" Rodney asked.

"Maybe this one will make it out of this ordeal," she said.

Holly pulls the trigger. The bullet explodes from the chamber, and blood erupts from the top of his skull. Blood splashes across Holly's face and the man drops in front of her, leaking splattered brain matter and crimson. The hooded men scream, but Holly grows angry.

"If you had known this would be the consequence, I would have my guns, and you all would have your lives. This isn't a time for begging. This is a time for dying. Never again," Holly said.

Holly wipes the blood from her eyes and reaches up for an assault rifle. Rodney stops her.

"Might I suggest something a little more subtle? Here." Rodney hands her a Desert Eagle handgun, which looks like a toy squirt gun in Rodney's hands but appears to be heavy machinery in the hands of Holly.

"My gift to you. I stole that from one of their other trucks," Rodney said.

"You are too kind, Rodney," Holly said with a smile on her face. It was the first time she'd looked at him with any romantic thoughts toward him. She maintained her composure and walked over to the men. "I think they deserve to see their last moments."

Holly pulled the hoods off of the three men. One was sobbing, while the other two tried to scream into the duct tape. She placed the handgun against one of their temples and pulled the trigger. The bullet pierced all three of their skulls, erupting in thick blood and brain fragments. All of their limp corpses fell to the ground in perfect sequence. She sighed and stood before Rodney, handing him back the gun.

"I love it," Holly said.

She entered the bathroom and washed her face of the blood. She dried it with a fresh towel Rodney had prepared for her. She reapplied her smeared makeup and walked toward the door.

"Same time next week?" Rodney asked. "I will be here," she said.

Rodney approached Holly and hugged her. She kissed his cheek and exited.

HOLLY WAS NEVER THE person to attract sizable crowds or blend into them. She strolled through the belligerent patrons that usually graced Friday night bars and paced faster. She made her way down several alleys until she found a small restaurant called Consume, almost hidden by piles of apartment trash and "for lease" covered storefronts.

"One for Holly," she said gracefully to the hostess.

"Good evening, Holly. Jeff, the chef, spoke kindly of you this evening. He was expecting your arrival. I will let him know you are here," the hostess said.

The hostess escorted Holly to her secluded seat. Holly peered across the dining room to see people of all uncommon types among attendance. Colorful misfits in white-collar clothing, elderly couples with concealed firearms, waiters and waitresses dressed in revealing attire were many of the patrons there tonight. It was a sight right out of

Holly's mind, and she wouldn't dare surround herself with any other group of people except her own.

"Holly, the Queen of Night. Is that still your formal title?" Jeff asked.

"It never was. Only a name from someone who didn't live too long. I do enjoy the irony, though," Holly said. Jeff sat next to Holly. He leaned in toward her, maintaining eye contact.

"You know, Holly, tonight is an extraordinary night. It is the 100th night I have served you. I find it to be an honor to have even met you," Jeff said. Holly leaned in closer. She smiled and gripped Jeff's hand.

"You know I have always been happy with how you treat me. Nothing but the utmost respect," Holly said.

Jeff peered back toward the kitchen and waved to one of his assistants. The server wheeled out a cart decorated with fine silver. A silver serving lid covered the dish. Holly looked closer with suspicion and enthusiasm, as she wasn't expecting such exceptional dining upon arrival. The cart arrived at the table, and Jeff dismissed the server. He uncovered the plate.

"A special dish for the magnificent Holly," Jeff said, smiling.

A thin cut of meat was lying on the plate, drenched in a sauce Holly didn't recognize. She poked at it gently with her fork, examining it.

"Is this... is this a new dish?" Holly asked.

"You could say that," Jeff said.

"What is it?" Holly asked with confusion. Jeff looked at her in surprise, as if she should know what it is. He peered across the restaurant, noticing people were staring, but weren't brave enough to keep eavesdropping. She looked across the room, and everyone was back to attending their meals and conversations. Jeff sat closer to Holly.

"You had requested this casually, in conversation, some time ago. I am fulfilling your wish," Jeff said with slight frustration in his voice.

"Can you remind me what that request was?" Holly asked.

"It is human," Jeff said.

Holly stared down at it, remembering the conversation clear as day the second that word left his tongue. She gazed upon it with excitement but overwhelming anxiety. Jeff placed his hand on her shoulder.

"You need not worry. I made sure it was a clean kill. No illnesses, no addictions. I prepared them as I would prepare any other fine meat. I assure you it is of the highest quality," Jeff said.

"Did you know who they were?" Holly asked.

"I know she was more suitable for where she is now, than the life we live," Jeff said, smiling. He stepped in front of Holly, bowing before gazing at her one last time. "Enjoy your meal."

"I must say that you certainly live up to your title," Holly said.

Jeff walked toward the kitchen and left Holly to feast. Holly tasted the meal, and it was everything she'd expected. Remembering how she'd started her night was an aid toward helping her pass any guilt she had upon seeing her dish. She dined alone, without a single person interrupting her exquisite meal.

THE PLATFORM WAS QUIET when Holly reached her regular waiting spot by the staircase. She could peer toward the stumbling drunks at the far end or admire the couple that was okay displaying their affection for one another in the depths of the city.

"Well, you are fine as fuck," a voice said in close proximity. An immature man eyed Holly with one thought rolling around in his head.

Several of his friends gathered close by, provoking his poor demeanor further. "Goddamn."

"You think so?" Holly asked.

"I sure do. What does it take to get someone like you?" the man asked.

Holly smirked. She placed her hair behind her ear and stepped closer to him. His friends whistled and cheered in the background as he licked his lips. Holly looked up at him.

"All I need is a quiet room to handle you," she said.

"Come on," he said eagerly, grabbing her wrist and pulling her to the nearby bathroom. He closed the door behind her, locking it. He threw his jacket and shirt to the counter. Holly carefully placed her handbag there, too. He approached her, gripping her waist and sliding his hand down to squeeze her ass.

"You think you can handle all of me? Everything I offer?" Holly asked.

"I do," he said. He slapped Holly's ass and slid his hands back up toward her chest. Holly backed up and moved toward the stall.

"Let's see what you got," Holly said. She backed into the stall, and he followed her in. She slid her hand under her skirt, smiling at him with luring eyes.

"Tell me you want it," Holly said as she lured him in with her eyes. He moved closer.

"I want it," he said, gently gripping her throat.

Holly smiled. She pulled her hand from beneath her skirt quickly. She drew a blade, jabbing him in the stomach several times. He stumbled back, falling into the sink. He struggled to get up while smearing blood all over the floor and counter.

"Stop, stop," he pleaded.

Holly raised her blade and swung it fiercely across his face. He wailed in pain. He tried crawling toward the door. Holly dug her heel into his back, pinning him down and causing more agony in the opening in his gut.

"Please stop. Why are you doing this?" he asked. Holly knelt to look him in the eye.

"You looked at me like an object as soon as I noticed you. The way you speak, touch me, all of it. Do you think you'd have mercy if I asked you to stop? If it's not me, it'll be someone else. You won't know how to stop until someone stops you. That someone will be me. Never again," Holly said.

Holly pressed her boot into his neck and held steady until the body beneath remained still. She rinsed her hands and blade of the evidence of her acts and adjusted her jacket, which hid the splatters of blood that got on her clothing. Holly applied another layer of lipstick before stepping past the corpse. She exited the bathroom and locked the door behind her. She walked toward the group of friends waiting to praise their friend.

"Sorry, guys, he didn't last as long as he expected," Holly said with a smile across on her face. The group broke down in loud laughter. She luckily caught the train doors as they were closing and peered toward the bathroom door as the group tried to open it.

The night drew toward its end as the massive crowds that once flooded the street were whittled down to the desperate souls trying to collect spare change, or stay composed from their intoxicating night. Holly waited as the train approached her station. She reached into her pocket and discreetly pulled out her knife. She looked at the side.

To the Queen. Love Rod.

She was never sure if Rodney had meant his signature as a crude metaphor, or if he wasn't able to spell. She was happy that his gift could keep her at peace tonight, and she was grateful to him.

IT WAS FOUR O'CLOCK in the morning as Holly unlocked her apartment door, dropping her bag and coat as if they'd weighed her down her entire life. She walked over to her living room wall and gazed at a giant collage of pictures she had been working on for several months. It illustrated photos of the beautiful city scenery, her career ambitions and personal goals, and a tiny newspaper article centered amid an artist's creative dream board.

ature ***Woman Survives Vicious Attack By Local Gang.***

Images of Holly's most horrific memory penetrate her mind. She recalls her screaming, several men surrounding her and taking something from her she could never get back. She removes her blood-stained shirt, revealing several scars scattered across her torso and arms. She places her knife on the coffee table and brushes her hair behind her ear. She takes several deep breaths and rips the article off of the wall, to make sure she's never reminded of it again.

"Never again," she whispered.

Holly made her way into the bedroom and collapsed, as if tearing the paper used the last ounce of strength she had. She looked out her window and saw the Saturday morning light coming toward her every second she allowed herself to stare. She let the exhaustion overcome her, as she knew Friday nights were nothing compared to her Saturdays.

10

Final Angel

Ben's ship approached the distant planet. Its moons decorated the planet's orbit, and meteors drifted slowly in the planet's gravity. Distant stars gleamed in the peripherals of the small world. Ben felt closer in his search as the radar identified the planet on his navigation.

"We have arrived, Ben," said Lady Cosmic, the navigation system. She was an upgrade to an earlier masculine model known as Navigator. Ben requested she be installed in his ship so he could converse with a woman. It was this journey he was on with Lady Cosmic that made it crucial for him to talk to a woman regularly.

"Time until we reach the surface?" Ben asked.

"Approximately twenty-two minutes," Lady Cosmic retorted.

"I hope she's down there. We have come so far to find her," Ben said. He pushed the throttle forward and hastened toward the remote planet. He was on a journey to find his lost love, Aileena. "I hope we find something."

"I hope so, too, Ben," Lady Cosmic said enthusiastically.

The ship touched down on the surface, and the thrusters went from a roar to a calm humming. The cockpit opened, and Ben dropped to stand on the surface. His slim suit protected him, but kept him agile for an active search. He walked several feet from his ship and peered around at his surroundings. The planet was calm.

"Lady Cosmic, launch searcher mode," Ben said.

"Searcher mode activated."

A chrome sphere dropped from the bottom of the ship and rolled to Ben's feet. The sphere expanded into multiple moving parts until it formed a body-like shape. The legs were long and slender, and the arms were slightly longer than Ben's average build. A head morphed out of the liquid metal torso, and a holographic screen emerged where a regular face would be.

Lady Cosmic towered over Ben, standing nearly seven feet tall. Her screen displayed a geographical scan of the nearby terrain for Ben to see. Lady Cosmic's head turned in a complete circle before returning to face Ben.

"Scan complete. Life forms detected in the distance. I am picking up a reading of a cloaking device," Lady Cosmic said.

"Can you override it?" Ben asked. A visualization of digital locks opening filled Lady Cosmic's screen. All the locks opened, and then something appeared to cover the ground for miles ahead of them.

"Complete," Lady Cosmic said, peering toward their alternative view of the darkened ground they stood on. Dead bodies were scattered across the area as far as their eyes could see.

"Someone slaughtered them. Who would do this to so many people?" Ben asked.

"Incoming. Get behind me," Lady Cosmic said.

Lady Cosmic quickly formed a barrier around Ben as an incoming blast pushed her back a few inches. Her neck and shoulder appeared badly damaged, but she flexed her arm and the metallic layer one may call skin glowed with a blinding light before appearing as if brand new.

Several beings rose from the blanket of corpses. They walked toward Ben and Lady Cosmic, drawing weapons that seemed to be of high caliber.

"Under no circumstances are you to intervene." Lady Cosmic opened her palm, and a black dome formed over Ben. A blast ricocheted off the dome. Lady Cosmic turned and faced the shooter.

"It would be wise to identify yourself before firing another shot," she scolded, flexing herself to intimidate the attackers.

"You are trespassing on land that now belongs to the Decimator. I will take you both prisoner and surrender your ship to our cause," the armed warrior said. He appeared to be their leader, as heavy armor decorated him and a layer of blood made Ben assume he'd performed most of the killing himself.

"I will ask you one more time to identify yourself," Lady Cosmic said. She widened her stance and extended her arms.

The army of now twenty warriors all chuckled in unison.

"I have cut through dozens of your robot bitch kind. We own you now. Don't let suicide be your last decision. We outnumber you." The leader cocked his rifle.

"By my calculations, you have a seventeen percent chance of victory. Do not engage, or I will use deadly force," she said. Lady Cosmic's screen displayed crosshairs. Her face glowed with a blinking red light. Ben and the warriors shielded their eyes from the glare. Several men dropped to the ground before they knew what happened. Some gripped at their necks to stop the bleeding, while others had noticeable holes in their foreheads from bullets erupting from Lady Cosmic.

"Fourteen hostiles remaining."

"Open fire!" The men raised their firearms like an orchestra beginning a song. Their lasers and bullets flew toward Lady Cosmic in a wave of desolation.

The leader looked down through his scope. He saw Lady Cosmic right in front of him before she sliced the barrel off of his rifle. She threw her face into his, shattering his nose. He let out a shriek before getting launched aggressively by her powerful legs. She made her way toward each warrior. She strategically executed them with brutal force. She crushed bones like tin cans. Blood coated her body like it was raining down from the sky. Ten hostiles remained.

Some of them got good shots in as they could, pushing her back with the blasts. She crushed or disassembled their weapons with a smile on her face before she turned her arm into a serrated blade. She took one hostile and cut from his collarbone down, and didn't stop until she cut through his opposite waistline. He was dead before she finished cutting, but her blade kept ripping flesh with her hostile mode activated. Seven hostiles remained.

She was merciful with some, cutting into their brains for a quick kill, then back to brutality for the final three. One emptied his entire magazine into her torso. Despite doing minor damage, she sliced him from side to side. He dropped to his knees, screaming while trying to hold his intestines in place. She grabbed and cocked the shotgun that rested in his arm, placed it against his forehead, and blew his head onto the ground and the remaining warriors. As the final two attempted to surrender, she beheaded them both.

"Are you okay?" Ben asked after watching her cut through them. She had looked defeated, but Ben never really understood how her outer shield was so powerful. She took on extreme damage like the average person took a wasp sting.

"I am. I still sustain eighty-nine percent of my armor."

Lady Cosmic noticed the leader had survived the attack as he crawled away from her. She approached him slowly. "I command you to halt, or you will force me to use further aggression."

He drew a sidearm and fired, emptying the clip into her. He hit her display screen, cracking the corner. He smiled as she covered her face.

"How's that feel, bitch?" the leader asked as he chuckled.

Lady Cosmic uncovered her face. The screen remained cracked, but she maintained functionality. She walked toward him slowly.

"I maintain ninety-three percent of my visibility," she said. She approached him and reached for his leg.

She twisted it, breaking it immediately. He let out a scream, and she lifted him by his armor. "Now, state your identity before your death comes quicker."

"My name isn't important. I am an officer of the Swarm Army. The elite fighting force of the Decimator. This planet is ours, and the next planet will be, too. Until we find The Final Angel, we will stop at nothing. When he finds what you did to us, he will do much worse to you and the boy."

"Speak of this Final Angel again," Lady Cosmic said.

"They say it's the unstoppable ship. It can outrun fleets, armor stronger than a planetary explosion, and you only see it when it's attacking. The Decimator wants it," the warrior said.

"Thank you. That will be all," Lady Cosmic said before gripping his neck with both of her hands and crushing it. She tossed his corpse several feet away. She walked over to Ben and deactivated Ben's shield.

"You haven't fought like that since our first week together," Ben said. "Like riding a bike, huh?"

"I have fought twice as many men, with twice as much strength. I must protect my leader at all costs."

Ben couldn't believe, even for someone incapable of emotion, anyone could remain calm after a battle meant for many androids. She walked ahead of him slowly, and he followed close behind. Lady Cosmic's screen expanded as she scanned the area. Her screen returned to its standard blank display. It glowed in and out.

"I am detecting a heavy frequency," Lady Cosmic said.

"Where?" Ben asked.

Lady Cosmic pointed toward the ground. They both looked at their feet and noticed the soil seemed as if it had been moved recently. A large circular plot of dirt contrasted with the green and brown grass. Ben reached to touch the fresh soil and buried his hand as far as it could go.

"It looks like someone buried something," Ben said.

"Stand back, Ben," Lady Cosmic said, the blaster built into her forearm emerging. It charged with a loud hum. Ben jumped out of the way. Lady Cosmic braced her wrist with her other hand and fired into the soil with a light blast. A wave of dirt covered them both. Lady Cosmic retracted her blaster, and metallic fingers emerged from her hand. She extended her arm to reach into the small crater.

Ben approached the edge and peered into the opening. Lady Cosmic pulled a white, luminescent cube from the crater. She placed it on the ground beside the hole. Ben approached it and admired it closely.

"I don't detect a threat toward you or your suit. Proceed."

Ben looked up at Lady Cosmic, hoping he looked as brave as she did. He gripped the cube on either side and lifted it from the ground. A blue beam shot out toward the sky and projected a holographic screen several feet above their heads. It activated a transmission.

Aileena emerged in front of the screen to record a personal message. Ben froze in place. It was the first time he had seen her face, excluding pictures, in several years. Her face, riddled with fear and concern, moved as she spoke.

"This is a distress call to those fleeing the Decimator and the Swarm Army. I have received the location of the Final Angel and have hidden the ship. It won't be long until they find me again. I am hiding this to make sure it doesn't fall into the hands of someone dangerous, but, instead, someone courageous. I hope whoever you are, whoever is seeing this, can use this information to fight back. To my fellow fighters of The Barricade, I will communicate with you when it is safe. To the people of this desolate planet, I hope I can one day thank you for aiding in my venture to keep the Final Angel in safe hands. To anyone, please join and fight toward ridding the galaxy of the Decimator. This is Aileena, commanding officer of The Barricade."

The video screen went blank. Ben's hopes escaped him, as Aileena was more distraught than she'd ever been. *Who was this Decimator she mentioned? How did she get involved? How did this Final Angel relate to her leaving Earth?*

"Was she the one you were looking for?" Lady Cosmic asked.

"Yes. That was Aileena. Despite her involvement in all of this chaos, I had hoped. Maybe, even the slightest chance-"

The screen illuminated again. Aileena emerged and stared directly into the camera.

"Ben. It's been a very long time. I hope you are the one who discovers this. I know you're the type who waits until the credits finish in movie theaters. That's why I left this for you. Anyone else would have turned it off by now. There is a lifetime of things I want to share with you, tell you, show you. Someday I will share them all with you. For now, I want you to know I am safe. The Final Angel is in my possession, and I am prepping it to take on the Decimator. When it is safe, we will have a chance in this universe. I love you. I love you and will always love you,you until the end of the starry sky. I will see you again. Goodbye, Ben."

Aileena wiped tears from her eyes and blew Ben a kiss. She smiled and ended the transmission. The light retracted into the cube, and it stopped glowing. Ben dropped the cube and tears ran down his face. Lady Cosmic approached him and picked up the cube.

"She remembered you," Lady Cosmic said.

"Yeah. Aileena knew it would be me."

"This is not just a transmitter, Ben. It is giving me coordinates, too." Lady Cosmic held the cube in between her palms and displayed a map on her screen. Ben stared in awe, wondering where it would lead. Hoping toward Aileena, he rushed to the ship and opened the cockpit. He started the ship.

"Lady Cosmic, launch Flight mode. Sync new coordinates in the destination," Ben yelled.

Lady Cosmic dissolved herself and the cube and merged into the ship's system. Her voice echoed in the ship's cockpit.

"Destination located. Ben, do you think it is wise to go? It could be a trap," Lady Cosmic said.

"She would lead me toward her. She will bring us somewhere safe," Ben said. The ship lifted from the surface and ascended into the atmosphere, guided by the distant stars growing brighter.

"We won't stop until it leads us to the Final Angel," Ben said.

"Ben, we are in search of the ship?" Lady Cosmic asked.

"No, we are in search of Aileena," Ben said. "Something tells me the ship was named after her."

Ben threw the throttle forward, blasting them into deep space.

11

WHERE TO GO TO FEEL NOTHING

Warren opened the car door for Claire and reached to help her. She accepted his hand, smiling, and stood up. He closed the door behind her, and they made their way toward the sidewalk. They crossed the street and looked down at the nearby park.

Warren couldn't help but admire Claire as she brushed the hair out of her face. She noticed his smile, returning one briefly. Her expression quickly turned to dread. She didn't have enough time to let the words escape her lips.

"Look-" she said.

BANG!

Warren went airborne and lost what reality he was enjoying. The sky was below him, and the ground was above him. Sound returned as he came closer to the ground. He fell hard onto the pavement, hitting his face. He heard something snap, and he felt the pain right behind it. Blood filled his mouth while it poured from his bottom lip.

Warren felt the world return as the usual sights he saw moments before came into focus. A scream broke the overbearing silence. He looked around as he struggled to raise himself up. There was the pain again—his wrist had snapped, exposing bone that breached the skin. Several minutes would go by before the deep gashes in his cheek and forehead would give off the same pain. Luckily, his adrenaline didn't let him feel it just yet.

Warren yelled out in agony. He was still for a moment before he tried his other wrist, giving himself leverage to look beyond his immediate field of vision. He knelt on one leg before pushing himself to his feet, which were miraculously unharmed.

"Claire? Claire!" Warren yelled. He saw people gathered around a wrecked car. A man walked up to Warren urgently.

"Hey, hey, buddy. Take it easy. You took a nasty fall," the man said.

"My fiancé. I don't see her. I need to find-" Warren said before something distracted him. He saw legs sticking out from beneath the car. He knew those shoes, and he knew those legs. He knew something was about to change his life.

"Hey, the ambulance is coming," the man said. Warren pushed past him. "Hey, let me help you!"

Warren didn't want to hear anything but Claire's voice. He rushed toward her. The crowd noticed. They stepped aside as if they were parting for him directly.

"Claire! Claire!" Warren yelled.

He approached the car. He looked into Claire's lifeless eyes.

Warren shot awake from his deep sleep. He wiped sweat from his face and caught his breath. He looked down at his heavily scarred wrist. He tried to block out the memory of recovering from the accident, but it still haunted him whenever he used his hand. He dragged the covers off himself and walked into the bathroom.

Warren washed his face and dried it carefully with a towel. He bent his wrist the wrong way.

"Ow, fuck!" Warren yelled. He dropped the towel on the sink, and it knocked some of his toiletries to the floor. Everything scattered around the room. He let out a frustrated sigh as he looked down at the scar tissue flexing his wrist and shuddering in pain. The haunting scars across his face stared back in the reflection that he refused to accept was his. He exited the bathroom and sat down in front of his television, flipping through the channels.

He looked at the clock—3:04 A.M.

"Warren? Warren!" someone yelled. Warren jumped from his sleep and looked around the group in the circle. The counselor seemed concerned.

"I assume it was another sleepless night, Warren?" the counselor asked. Warren nodded as he tried waking himself up, sitting up straight in the chair.

"It's been constant lately. Probably because the anniversary was last month," Warren said, trying to fight back the urge to cry. "Sorry, it's still fresh to me."

"It can feel like it happened yesterday for many people. We are all here grieving over loved ones, ourselves, and each other. The key is not to lose sight of reality. We are recovering from the trauma and progressing to a normal life, the normal life we used to have. We are all on our way. Same time on Friday, everyone. Have a wonderful evening," the counselor said.

The counselor smiled at Warren. Hardly able to, Warren worked up a fake smile, which they both knew he had forced. The group stood up and exited. Warren walked toward his car. He fiddled with his keys and reached for the door.

"Warren, hey, wait up!" said Howard. An overweight gentleman, Howard Howard, shuffled over to Warren as fast as he could. He caught his breath and then reached in to shake Warren's hand.

"Hey, Warren, how are you?"

"Hey, Howard. Fine, I guess," Warren said.

"Great session tonight. I can feel more positivity radiating through me. It helps the healing," Howard said excitedly. His smile wasn't as contagious as he had hoped. "I heard you mention you haven't been sleeping well."

"That's right," Warren said.

"Well, I have a suggestion for you," Howard said. "What is it?" Warren asked.

"Here." Howard reached into his pocket and pulled out a small container with pills rattling around in it. He grinned as Warren looked at him in confusion.

"They're over the counter, I swear. Sleeping pills, but they're much stronger," Howard said, handing them over to Warren.

"Have you tried them?" Warren asked.

"Yeah. They work like a charm. Even for a big guy like me," Howard said, chuckling with his wheeze-filled laugh.

"Thanks. I'll probably need it tonight," Warren said. He slid the container into his pocket.

"Be sure to tell me how you feel on Friday. Goodnight, Warren."

"Goodnight, Howard."

After a quiet dinner and some poorly scripted T.V. that he just couldn't turn away from, Warren was comfortable in his bed. He opened the container Howard had given him, noticing the pills were an unusually bright green color. He shrugged it off and swallowed them down.

Warren faded into his exhaustion. His eyes finally closed, and he drifted off to sleep.

"Warren. Come on."

A familiar voice made Warren jump. It's Claire. Could it be? No, it's not possible. She's gone. She passed thirteen months ago. He was sure it was her voice. No one else sounded like Claire.

"No, no, it can't be," Warren whispered. Warren wouldn't accept it as Claire. The voice was right next to him, breezing against his skin like a frigid night's night wind. A hand gripped his shoulder. His eyes opened, and he looked up, and Claire was sitting at the side of his bed. She smiled at him.

"I'm here, Warren. It's okay. Don't be afraid," Claire said.

Even though Warren wanted nothing more than to speak to her after her death, this moment held nothing but dread. Everything seemed transient, which he couldn't figure out.

"You aren't Claire. You aren't here at all," Warren said frantically.

"Don't be silly. It's me. Let's go," Claire said calmly.

"Go where?" Warren asked with concern.

"Wherever we want to go. Here, you don't have to feel anything you don't want to. Eddie and I have so much fun. We can all have fun together," she said. Claire turned toward the doorway, and an adolescent boy stood in the shadows, waving at Warren. Unable to find his words, Warren stared back at Claire with a foreboding feeling.

"Claire, who is that?" Warren asked.

"Eddie, I want you to meet my fiancé. It's all right, don't be shy." Claire waved Eddie over as soon as she finished speaking.

The boy, hidden in the shadows, emerged into the light. Immediately, Warren knew this entire encounter felt wrong. The adolescent boy had blood splattered down his face, and a sizable hole at the top of his forehead. The boy stopped when he was in plain sight of both Claire and Warren. He waved at Warren.

"Hello. My dad told me about you. Claire makes sure I'm okay," Eddie said.

"Who? Who is your dad?" Warren asked.

"Warren, we look after one another here. Howard lets me know how you're doing. It's good here. We can be together—the four of us. I want us to be a family," Claire said.

Warren shuddered down into his bed, shaking his head violently. He covered his eyes.

"No, no, no. Stop. I don't want to be here anymore," Warren said.

Claire gripped his shoulders tightly. She leaned in and whispered to him.

"Warren, don't you want to be with me again?" Claire asked. Warren looked up, and she smiled at him. In an instant, her neck snapped back with an aggressive symphony of crackles and pops. A loud crack echoed throughout the room. Her head locked in place, facing the ceiling. Warren looked down at her hands as they turned ghostly white.

"Claire!" Warren yelled.

Warren shot up from his deep sleep. The morning sun blinded him as he came back to reality from his dread-filled nightmare. *Was it real? Was she here?* It felt so real. He knew everyone exaggerated when they talked about their nightmares.

This was different. It was transient and real, all at once. It wasn't a dream; it happened. The only thing Warren was sure of at that moment was he would make sure Howard thoroughly explained himself before Warren allowed him to go home.

Friday came and Warren anxiously attended his group meeting. He hadn't stopped thinking about his experience, or at least that's what he called it. From the moment they sat down, it was nothing but white noise.

Warren locked his focus onto Howard and couldn't budge, no matter what. Even the counselor calling his name several times wasn't enough to crack him. They kept moving along the group, as was routine. Warren wasn't a stranger to skipping his turn — especially when Claire first died.

Warren rushed out before everyone else and waited by Howard's car. He planned to do so all week, to make sure Howard couldn't escape the conversation. As if he were expecting to have a confrontation, Howard smiled when he saw Warren waiting for him.

"Quite the experience, huh, Warren?" Howard asked, chuckling.

Warren wanted to punch him with every bit of energy he'd stored that week. Speaking with Claire was everything Warren had hoped for since he first saw her underneath the car. Howard chuckling about it like it was some unpleasant drug trip could be the worst way to get a friend out of Warren.

"Howard, I need you to explain what the fuck that was. No jokes, no tricks. Just tell me," Warren said.

"Gee, Warren, that's one hell of an icebreaker," Howard said before he felt Warren's hands swiftly push into his ample gut, knocking him into his car. Howard stopped laughing, and his smile drained immediately to intense concern.

"Let me clarify that we aren't friends. You tell me or I'll let the counselor know you're handing out mystery pills in the parking lot," Warren said.

Howard straightened himself up. He adjusted his jacket and then reached into his pocket for his keys.

"Come on, let me buy you some food. I'm starving," Howard said.

"I'm not hungry," Warren scolded.

"It's the least I can do for making you angry. It'll take a little while to explain, anyway," Howard said. He opened the car door and hopped in. He started the engine while Warren stood where he was. Howard waved him in with a friendly gesture. Warren didn't want to, but he knew the answer was somewhere in the night's journey with Howard.

The drive was grueling for Warren. Howard's constant small talk faded out into a white noise strain. Warren could only gaze out into the night, lit by nearby excitement. He was mesmerized by couples dining on decadent food and families exploring the flourishing shopping possibilities, as he sat alongside someone who had just turned his thoughts to mush. A cold emptiness overcame him as he continued to glare at the hope he knew he couldn't save anymore.

They entered the diner and sat in the back. Warren felt more comfortable not being around people if he had to snap at Howard. He was doing his best not to erupt in public. He stuffed his face with the overabundance of food he'd ordered, since Howard had generously offered to pay.

"About seven years back, my son Eddie passed away. He was always so excited to see me when he got home from school. One afternoon, I had just got back from the shooting range and was properly storing my things away. I left it out for only a moment to open the locker. I turned around, and he was holding it. My little Eddie had the gun gripped in his hands. Then he just looked down into at it. I couldn't breathe. I couldn't move. Maybe if I had, he wouldn't- maybe he wouldn't have…"

Howard's eyes watered simultaneously with his quivering chin. He covered his eyes momentarily and composed himself. Warren couldn't eat. Not because he sympathized with Howard. He could picture Eddie vividly from his "experience". The blood splatter, the exit wound, and Eddie's haunting smile were as clear to Warren as they were to Howard when the incident happened in front of him.

"Sorry," Howard said, wiping his face with a napkin. "The one time I didn't check my gun before leaving and it cost me my son."

"You have nothing to be sorry about, Howard. I want to know what that pill was. What exactly was I seeing?" Warren asked.

"You saw my son and your fiancé," Howard said.

Warren couldn't believe that he was so blunt about it. Had Howard gone through the same experience? Warren dropped his utensils and leaned in.

"Is that what your magic drug does?" Warren asked sternly.

"I didn't believe it at first, either. After Linda left me, I had nothing else to lose. Some crappy pill that could make me see the dead? It seemed silly until I tried it. I got to hold my boy again. I said everything I wanted to say to him. I want to be with him again more than anything," Howard said.

Warren couldn't believe what he was hearing. He tried to keep a curious look on his face, even though he couldn't stop thinking how crazy Howard was.

"You can't. Your son is gone. I don't understand how we are seeing them, but this isn't healthy. We need to make more progress. We are still grieving," Warren said.

"Warren, we are all going to die one day. Fifty years from now in our sleep, or tomorrow morning by an armed robber. My son was my entire life. I can be a part of a family again. You and Claire can be a family again." Howard reached into his pocket and pulled out two more pills. He locked eyes with Warren as if the next words were the most important thing he would ever say.

"I think Sunday night will be my last night alive. I'd like you to consider the same."

Warren sat back in his seat. His heart pounded in his chest, and his breathing became scarce. He felt the devoid glare piercing through his mind, as if Howard already knew his answer. Warren didn't even know his answer. Warren knew nothing at all at that moment.

"How could you even suggest something like that? Seriously, what is wrong with you?" Warren's stunned expression escalated to anger swiftly. He got closer to Howard again.

"I've never had a better idea in my life. It all goes away. For both of us," Howard said, reaching over and giving Warren the two pills. "Claire would want you at her side. Give it some thought tonight. I'll wait until you are ready, so we can be with them together. Finish up, and I'll give you a ride back to your car."

Howard stood up and pulled a one-hundred-dollar bill out of his pocket. He placed it carefully under his glass and smiled kindly at Warren before walking out of the diner. They had exhausted the night for one small yet disastrous conversation.

WARREN KEPT REPEATING HOWARD'S words in his head during the ride home. He walked into his home, nearly tripping on several pieces of furniture, and still contemplated the horror Howard proposed while he lay in bed. The darkness in his house was equally as soothing as it was lonely. He could contemplate Howard's words while realizing he was alone every night.

Every night he missed Claire—but ever since his "experience"—it has only heightened his desperation for a solution. Could Howard be serious about this? Was he ready for us both to give in? Warren thought. He had known Howard for months, but didn't speak to him until the last few weeks.

Warren had tried the pill, and it worked. But how? He never quite got that answer. He wasn't sure if Howard even knew. Was he right, though? Was there no other reason to wake up? Warren didn't socialize with anyone else. Most of Warren's thoughts were getting out of work, dealing with his loss in therapy, and Claire.

Claire.

He missed Claire. He longed for Claire. To hold her, kiss her, and love her again was everything he wanted. For the last thirteen months, those were the only thoughts rattling around in Warren's brain. If only he could speak to her again. I can.

Warren swallowed down one pill and closed his eyes. He shifted his body and felt as if the arms of grief dropped him, falling for what felt like several minutes, and the bed was his salvation. His eyes were still closed when Warren felt Claire's hand touch his leg. He reached out and grabbed it as he opened his eyes. She smiled at him.

"Hey there," she whispered.

"Claire, I don't know what to do. Is giving up the right decision?" Warren asked.

"The right choice is the one that brings you happiness," Claire said. "Being together will make us happy."

"That is the only thing I've wanted every day since..." Warren struggled to speak as tears filled his eyes.

Claire smiled. She reached her hands out. "Let us help you," Claire said.

Eddie walked in from the darkness like the first time. The exit wound on his forehead was illuminated by the minimal light the night offered. He also extended his hands out.

"Let us help you," Eddie said. Warren tried his best not to show his expression as he struggled to look at the boy.

"Let us help you," a third voice said. Warren looked around briefly and saw nothing besides the empty darkness of his bedroom. It echoed around his room. Claire and Eddie remained still, as if they hadn't heard it. A shadowy figure stepped in behind Eddie and reached down toward him, kissing the top of his head. From the darkness, the shadow became Howard, sauntering toward Warren.

"Howard?" Warren asked, raising the sadness and concern in his eyes.

"Warren, let us help you," Howard said, extending his hands out toward Warren. It was hardly visible, but Warren could see the bloodstains on Howard's cuffs. He reached out and slid Howard's sleeves up, exposing deep gashes in Howard's wrists. The blood was flowing out and drenching the sleeves even further. Howard still maintained his smile. Warren sat back in his bed.

As if his vision were extended with this frighteningly strong yet mysterious pill, Warren saw the entire room in a wide-angle. Howard on his left, Eddie in the center, and Claire on his right. All six arms extended, smiles all around, and the weirdly gruesome injuries that had placed these three individuals before Warren.

"Let us help you," said all three in unison.

Warren let out a horrified scream that he hoped would wake him up. It did. Warren bolted up with intensity. His entire body was soaked in sweat so severely that he wasn't sure someone hadn't drenched him with water. Relieved the morning light would ease his tension, his breathing gradually slowed as he stood and made his way to the bathroom. He stared in the mirror for several seconds, contemplating the horrific moments he'd just endured. He didn't wait for me.

Not sure if he was more shocked or lonely, he knew that the one person who had given him tangible hope recently had given up. Howard had gone without Warren. Mostly, it angered Warren. He thought about the hope that he saw taken from him by the same hand that gave it. The second pill rested on the edge of the sink.

In one swift move, Warren flicked it and watched it bounce around the porcelain before it dropped into the drain. The clicking sound as it fell deeper gave Warren the satisfaction he'd missed for a long time. He drew the faucet and reached for his toothbrush.

The group gathered their chairs together and opened them up in a semicircle. The counselor walked in and sat rather quickly.

"Before we begin, I'd like to bring something to everyone's attention," the counselor said. "A few nights ago, Howard took his own life. Now, this entire group is here to progress through loss, grief, pain, whatever it may be. His decision doesn't reflect us as people who want to heal, but someone who chose not to want to face it anymore."

Warren's hand shot up to interrupt the counselor. "Yes, Warren?" the counselor asked.

"I'd like to speak first today, if that's all right with everyone," Warren said boldly. The counselor smiled, and the rest of the group shifted in Warren's direction.

Warren knew that Howard was honest in about his intentions to benefit them both. Warren even knew that Howard didn't mean to abandon him in his choice. However, Warren knew that it wasn't his time to go.

He looked at these people and saw what he saw every morning when he glanced quickly at himself in the mirror, or the intentional stare when he wanted to. There was still pain, but there was hope. Hope would thrive later.

12

Feeding

Carter opened the car door for Heather before climbing in the tiny, beat-up, used car he had bought several weeks ago for half of his life savings. It ran, but it was an eyesore.

"Don't worry about the car. It gets us where we need to go," Heather said.

"I know. I just wish it was a better first impression for meeting your family." Carter was confident that their first impression of Carter would be the same as how they felt about his car—needs plenty of help and a miracle to make it last.

"My family cares about tradition, respect, and legacy. They couldn't care less about how your car looks.

Besides, it brings more personality to you." Heather was much more optimistic than Carter even imagined being. Still, he knew she was right. He would have to face them, whether with his crappy, beat-up car or in a brand-new Lamborghini. They pulled up to

Heather's home and got out. Heather gripped Carter's forearm as they approached the front door.

"Just be yourself. I know they'll love you," Heather said, reassuring Carter.

Carter scoffed. "As long as they don't look in the driveway."

Heather pushed the door open and let Carter in. She took off her shoes right away. Carter slid his shoes off and immediately felt hit by the heat in the room. He felt as if he'd stepped into a sauna or was leaning against a brick oven. He took his jacket off quickly.

"Mom, we're here," Heather exclaimed loudly.

"Wow, it's hot in here," Carter said as sweat dripped from his forehead.

Heather's mom walked in, almost as if she came directly to respond to his statement.

"Sorry, dear, we've been baking all day, and the oven fan isn't the best these days. How are you, sweetie?" Heather hugged her mom,mom Molly, tightly.

She whispered something into Heather's ear, but he couldn't hear it. She turned to him with a wide smile.

"It's nice to meet you, Carter. Heather can't stop talking about you." Molly reached in and hugged Carter, but not the same way she'd hugged Heather. This was more of a comforting, apologetic hug. He didn't know how to respond, but assumed she was trying to be friendly.

"Please come in. Let me introduce you to the rest of the family," Molly said.

Molly gripped Carter's arm firmly. Not enough to concern him, but enough to know she was eager to lead him. Heather followed him with the smiling face she'd had when she walked in. They entered the dining room, and Carter noticed two women. One was an innocent-looking younger girl with basic features about her.

This has to be Heather's sister, he thought. The other woman was a mystery to him.

Carter stared at this heavy, frightening-looking woman. Not only was she distant from the beauty that ran in Heather's family, but she was probably the ugliest woman Carter had ever seen before. She looked grouchy and was staring off into space — hypnotized by her thoughts.

"I'd like you to meet my sister, Stacey, and my aunt, Agnes," Heather said.

An ugly name to fit the face, Carter thought. As if she heard his thoughts, Agnes locked eyes with Carter. Her pupils were the blackest he'd ever seen. He felt like she was feeding on his soul. She smiled wickedly.

"Hello!" Stacey exclaimed. She ran over to hug Carter tightly. Her hug broke the trance he was in with Agnes, and Carter hugged her back. He approached Agnes with his hand extended.

"Hello, I'm Carter. It's nice to meet you," Carter said. Agnes scoffed. Carter wanted to give it back to her since it was naturally his reaction. Still, he kept his composure. Molly intervened for him.

"Agnes, you could at least be polite. I'm sorry about her, Carter. She gets grumpy on some of her medications," Molly said.

"It's no problem at all," Carter said.

"I hope you're hungry. I prepared quite the feast for you," Molly said enthusiastically.

"I appreciate that," Carter said, approaching the table.

The family gathered at the table while Molly brought the food out. A feast resembling Thanksgiving decorated the table. Carter thought it was unusual to have such a large meal just to meet him, but he wouldn't complain, since his empty stomach was howling. He watched the steam radiate from every dish and was anxiously waiting to fill his empty plate.

"This all looks delicious, Molly," Carter said.

Molly smiled. "Thank you, sweetie. No need to wait any longer. Let's eat."

The family dished out portion after portion. Carter kept eating as if he was trying to get his next fix of an addictive substance. Every bite seemed like the best experience, but it still wasn't enough.

Some casual conversation bounced around the table. Molly asked Carter and Heather about school before Molly discussed her work life. Everyone laughed, smiled, and showed enthusiasm, like Carter was already a member of the family.

Agnes stayed quiet, but maintained a sharp focus on listening to Carter.

"Any plans for the summer, Carter?" Molly asked.

"Not really. Mostly working and trying to get a better car," Carter said.

Agnes scoffed. "It is an eyesore." "Be nice, Agnes," Molly said.

"It's just an observation," Agnes sneered. She buried her face back into her plate.

"The car rides great; it just needs a facelift," Heather said. She smiled at him for reassurance.

"It gets me where I need to go," Carter said, peering out the window at his unsightly yet reliable car.

Dinner quickly finished as everyone devoured the food. Molly began cleaning up while Carter, Heather, and Stacey talked at the table. Agnes stayed quiet while staring into space.

"Girls, could you help me for a moment?" Molly asked. Stacey and Heather excused themselves and left Carter to sit across from Agnes.

She looked up, noticing she was alone with Carter. She scoffed at him again.

"So, how are you related-"

"Save it, boy. We both know you're here just to get in Heather's pants. Save me the small talk and let's get on with the evening." Agnes took a deep breath and retreated to her long gaze into nothing.

Carter couldn't believe what he'd just heard. He wanted to respond, but he was at a loss for words. Luckily, the rest of the family returned to the table. Molly carried pie in a dish.

"I hope you're still hungry, Carter," Molly said happily.

Heather and Stacey were smiling. Carter was speechless and still couldn't find any words once he saw the pie Molly placed on the table.

Carter felt heat from the pie like the first moment he'd entered the home. Sweat dripped from his forehead. The smell hypnotized him. After a feast, he didn't expect to be hungry, but the smell of the pie made him feel like he'd been starving for days.

"Heather told me your favorite flavor was apple pie," Molly said.

Carter didn't recall ever talking about pie with Heather. He served himself and had never tasted a pie as good as this one. Each bite tasted better than the one before. One slice led to two, and then a third. He finally felt full, despite each bite weakening him to the taste.

"Wow, that was delicious," Carter said. "Probably the best pie I've had in my life."

They all smiled at him, and it began to make him uncomfortable. Agnes sighed again. She reached over, grabbing the pie server and dug it deeply into Carter's hand.

"AHHHH!" Carter yelled out as blood poured from his hand.

Agnes broke her frown and finally smiled at him.

"Come on, Carter. Eat up. I like my boys with full bellies!" Agnes said maniacally. She laughed hysterically.

Molly placed her hand on Carter's shoulder. He looked up at her while he squirmed in his seat. "It's okay, dear," Molly said, "it's okay. You'll be just fine."

"Carter, it's okay. The whole family likes you," Heather said. "Much more than the last boy I brought home. My aunt has to eat, though."

Carter's eyes expanded in terror. Heather smiled at him kindly. Carter looked back at his hand, which had now gone numb. Blood poured from his palm, trickling down the table and dripping down to his pants. Agnes smiled as she leaned closer to Carter.

"Let's see how you taste, boy!" Agnes yelled.

Her eyes glowed white, and her jaw extended wider and wider. Carter couldn't help but look deep into Agnes' mouth. He saw the back rows of her teeth extend from the roof of her mouth. Bits of food dripped onto the table and into his lap went unnoticed as her mouth extended further and further.

He had frozen in place. Her mouth finally stopped stretching, and she froze above him. Carter was still stunned with fear; he noticed something about her eyes. The blinding white faded to a gray and then quickly to black.

"Heather, please, what is going-"

Agnes swung down swiftly and swallowed Carter's head whole. Her teeth latched into onto his neck, and she tore with great strength. Bone crunched, and skin shredded, separating the neck from the shoulders completely. Carter's body dropped to the floor and bled into the carpet. Agnes chewed and swallowed down her mouthful of skull and spine. Her jaw slowly returned to its average size.

"Goodness, this is quite a mess. Stacey, will you help me get this into the kitchen?" Molly said, reaching down to pick up Carter's body.

"Yes, Mom," Stacey said, gripping Carter's ankles and lifting him simultaneously with Molly.

Molly and Stacey walked out of the room and into the kitchen. Heather reached for her phone in her front pocket and pulled it out to see a new text from Jesse.

"Mom, Jesse said he would come over for dinner tomorrow!" she said excitedly. "Aunt Agnes, does that sound good to you?"

"I wish they weren't as stupid as this one, but whatever it takes to get a meal. It's like I can taste how useless they are," Agnes said.

"Oh, don't be so dramatic," Heather said, rolling her eyes. "I'll clean up the rug."

Molly chopped up the remains of Carter, and Heather cleaned up what had dropped on the floor with a towel and rug cleaner. The night became as normal as any other household on the street was after the family concluded dinner. Agnes staggered out of her seat and waddled toward the stairs.

"Molly, bring me leftovers!" Agnes shouted, heading up the stairs.

Carter would feed them for the rest of the week, and ignorantly fill Jesse's stomach tomorrow, right before the family had him for dinner.

13

All Was Quiet

THE ENTIRE CITY WAS in a sound vacuum. If there were anyone else alive, it would be a long time before Noah knew as he emerged from his bathtub. He knew it would be the safest place, and he was right. He looked outside directly from where his bathroom was, since the face of his building, now missing from the other three walls, let in a burst of dust and sunlight. He could tell the premises for the next three blocks were the same way.

He walked to the exposed opening and peered outside. Most of the city was nothing but mounds of cement and steel. The only sounds he heard were creaking from the demolished buildings, and the remaining glass giving way to gravity. There was a dense cloud of smoke in the distance as the city continued to fall from the damage. It became louder as he walked further outside.

CRACK!

Storefronts continued to crumble.

CRUNCH!

Large furniture plummeted to the ground from higher floors.
SMASH!
Plates of glass fell from everywhere. It was hard to keep track of where they dropped had dropped from, but none of of them had struck Noah yet, so he was okay with it for now. A thunderous roar made Noah freeze in place. He saw the monster finally rest at the edge of the city. It sat down like a tired athlete after a vigorous game.

It had won, but it had taken a beating from the military. Noah walked toward the nearby village square and climbed up the now decimated monument of a former president. He looked out at the monster as it recouped from the fierce battle, watching it bleed a dark blue color from its chest, four arms, and neck. One of its six eyes bled from being shot out by a missile. Still, it had won. Noah almost felt bad for the monster, but he knew his life had had more damage done to it than the monster had.

Noah stepped down and began walking the streets for some answers. Three tanks nearby lay flat, crushed in, or melted. Military trucks had a dark liquid coating, from being in the creature's blood, or were flattened by its wounded feet. The only things he saw to pick up nearby were severed limbs, or keys to cars under fallen slabs of cement.

The wind echoed loudly in the large openings throughout the buildings. Noah could hear the brisk air dancing around the destruction. It was the only thing that Noah found soothing in all of this wreckage. The rumbling and creaking grew louder in the distance, like an alarm clock past its time.

Smoke and debris filled the street. Noah witnessed a building seeing its last moments. It toppled and fell to the road, exploding,exploding; the sound echoing across the city. A cloud of dust filled the surrounding air. He quickly entered another building to avoid breathing in the dust.

The wave passed through the buildings. Clouds filled the street level floors as it moved swiftly down the street. Noah felt it breeze past him while he buried his face in his shirt. The combination of ash and dust covered him with a light layer, like he was in a snowstorm. He tried not to open his eyes, fighting every urge to. He glanced up slightly, and all he could see was a dense cloud. The dust wouldn't completely settle for another hour.

The creaking finally settled, and Noah had only silence again. He opened his eyes to see a faint haze in front of him. He could see into the street, but no further than half a block down. The bakery where he got his favorite cookies was still on fire. Someone had driven through the coffee shop he loved to stop at before work, and their corpse dangled out of the windshield. Noah even recognized the guy as someone he talked to every week.

Am I the only person still alive? he thought. He stepped forward, toward the entrance, and began searching again.

The monster still sat in the same spot, tending to its wounds. Noah looked into every building that he passed. No signs of life at all. If there weren't body parts scattered around, all he saw was blood beneath large piles of rubble or cars. He panicked.

I really might be the only one left, he thought. The monster stood up proudly. It looked down at its destruction and let out a loud shriek. It had won, and Noah was sure the monster knew that, too.

For a moment, they locked eyes. Noah wasn't sure if the monster was looking at him directly, but it felt like it was. Almost as if Noah took some glory away from the monster. Its eyes glowed. Noah froze. The monster inhaled like it was a big kid trying to imitate a mighty animal. Noah had heard that sound before. He ran into the nearest building and ducked beneath a pile of cement and bent steel.

The monster exhaled. A large beam shot out of its mouth. The beam gave off a piercing ringing sound as it cut into the remains of fallen skyscrapers. Glass shattered, while more debris pummeled to the ground at a scorching temperature. The monster walked forward and gave its full energy to the beam. It cut down every building below twenty floors and decorated the street with liquified steel and piles of lava.

Cars melted inward, and the city streets collapsed down to the subway platforms. The monster closed its mouth, and the beam ended its reign of devastation. The monster roared and sat back down.

Noah heard the echo of the monster thumping onto the ground. He knew the attack was over. Unless the monster planned on melting every bit of the remaining buildings, it was clear it had made its last move. Noah looked around the rubble that kept him safe and saw a car drop into the new opening in the street. The loud thud it made echoed down several blocks. The silence would soon consume Noah's ears again.

He carefully stepped out into the street once more—hiding behind piles of debris and destroyed cars—to avoid even the slightest attention. He didn't know which direction would bring him safety, but he kept going. He stopped for a moment to weigh his options. He could steadily move to the edge of the city and wait for some rescue team, or he could wait to see if the monster would ever leave.

It was at that moment Noah noticed a pair of eyes staring right at him. He saw from across the street as a girl—about his age—slowly emerged from the pile of rubble where she'd found solace. She stood, glaring, fixated on Noah.

"Hey, is it safe?" she asked softly, but loud enough for Noah to hear her from across the street. He peered over to see if it alarmed the monster, but it still sat there, resting or biding its time for something new to emerge.

"Yeah, come on over." Noah waved her over, and she swiftly made her way across the street.

She grew more beautiful as she got closer, Noah thought. He already felt it hard to concentrate on the city behind him when a beautiful girl was approaching him. She was nearly in reach before she dropped to her knees. Noah reached down to help her up when he noticed the large wound on the right side of her head.

Blood soaked her hair and drenched her ear. She looked up at him, smiling, unaware of how bad her injury was. Noah wrapped his arm around her and had her lean on the wall behind her. Her eyes didn't focus on him, which made him worry further.

She touched his shoulder, bracing herself. "Thank you for helping me."

"You're welcome. I'm Noah." Noah embraced her. He wasn't sure if it was more because of the attraction than her need for it, but he was glad not to be alone anymore.

"I'm... I'm..." she said, struggling to find her words. "Elly."

"Do you remember anything from before this happened, Elly?" Noah asked, peering out of their hideout toward the monster. "Anything at all?"

"I was with my mom and sister. One second we were at the dinner table, and the next moment I'm dangling from six floors up, and they'd already fallen to the ground," Elly said.

Noah knew anything she would say would be worse than his. He had just blown off a family party out of frustration. He didn't want to see people who would always ask about why he didn't have a wife, or a girlfriend, or why his career wasn't further along. Then he almost got blown up by a monster in his apartment. Noah wasn't a religious man, but after last night, he was reconsidering.

"What about you? Were you with family?" Elly asked. "No, I was home by myself," Noah said regretfully. "Do you think the military is coming?" Elly asked.

"They did, and they lost rather quickly." Noah didn't want her to notice the melted tank down the block, but it was only a matter of time before she saw.

"What do we do?" Elly asked.

"I'm trying to think of something. If that thing sees us, it'll blast us. If we stay here, we could get trapped or crushed in one of these buildings," Noah said.

Noah didn't know if it was karma or a mere coincidence, but pieces of cement plummeted to the ground as he spoke. It broke apart, and pieces flew all over the place. Noah stood in front of Elly to block her from the falling debris. He tried not to react when pieces flew into his back, but it hurt him more than he wanted to show. She smiled at him.

"Thank you. You didn't have to block me," Elly said.

"Don't mention it," Noah said.

The monster roared. Elly looked up, and Noah stood quickly, peering out from behind the wall and seeing it in the distance. It extended its arms, roaring in a victorious call to no one else.

"I think it knows it won," Elly chuckled.

"Yeah, no reason to think otherwise," Noah said.

The roaring slowly descended to an echo among the crippled buildings. The sound bounced from building to building, rattling loose pieces of glass to fall and break on the ground. Some fragments of concrete dropped near Noah and Elly. Noah reached over to Elly, helping her to her feet.

"Come here, let's get you further away from this," Noah said. Elly latched onto Noah's shoulder, grasping him firmly with her weakening grip. Noah placed her down in a corner between a wall that was still standing strong and an eight-foot slab of concrete.

"You'll be safe here. I will take another look outside."

"Please be careful, Noah," Elly said, reaching to grab Noah's hand. In any other circumstance, Noah normally shuddered away from a girl like Elly, being as insecure as he was. However, he knew it was in his benefit, and equally his responsibility, to be strong for Elly in her current state. He peered over the wall again to see the monster—back to tending to its wounds—while the city remained in its battlefield condition.

A distant rumbling sound came from the far side of the city. Noah noticed three fighter jets approaching rapidly toward the resting destroyer. They were in a perfect triangular formation as they approached the decimated city. One fighter jet broke the formation and flew toward the monster faster than the other two. It sprayed the monster with high caliber bullets. They bounced off the creature with only a paltry number of bullets piercing already-open wounds. The monster roared.

The second jet shot a missile at the monster. The monster turned its back to the oncoming missile, striking it with intense force. A sound wave shot over the city, echoing a loud bang throughout the wreckage. The monster roared in pain. It spun around, glaring at the oncoming third jet. The monster puffed up its chest and let out a beam from its mouth, no different from the one that had nearly killed Noah.

The jet, unable to avoid the oncoming blast, flew straight into it. It cut a sizable hole over the top of the jet, splitting the pilot in half, and scorching the back half of the aircraft. It plummeted toward the ground and crashed into a building. The explosion caught Noah's eye since it leveled what remained standing of the building. The other two jets circled to put some distance between themselves and the monster.

The monster rose to its feet, extending its arms and puffing up its chest. It let out another roar. A roar Noah hadn't heard since he flew across his apartment from the blast twelve hours earlier. He quivered in fear and ducked down, looking back at Elly.

"Two jets are attacking it. One already crashed," Noah said.

"Just three came?" Elly asked.

"Yeah, but they hurt it. Pissed it off more, though," Noah said.

"I'd like to see," Elly said. She pushed herself off the wall as she attempted to stand. She dropped to her knees. Noah rushed over to help her.

"Hey, you're better off sitting. That wound looks nasty," Noah said.

"Then why don't you look for something to make it better?" Elly asked.

Noah smiled at her retort. "Stay here. Don't go fighting that thing without me."

Elly smiled. "I'll tap in soon, but hurry back. I'm getting dizzy."

Noah sat Elly down again and walked across the street toward a market that seemed decent enough to raid.

Noah walked into the market and immediately climbed over the fallen shelves that had cracked through the main window. He headed toward the back of the store, where he knew the pharmacy was. Peering over the counter, he saw bandages, peroxide, and cleaning wipes to aid Elly. He bundled them up in his arms and walked toward the entrance. He passed the cooler and grabbed several bottles of water.

BOOM!

An explosion rocked the windows and threw items from the shelves. Noah saw pieces of burning shrapnel fly down the street. He peeked out the entrance of the market to see another jet taken down by the monster. The cockpit popped open from the flames, and the nose was crushed in from the impact. One wing dangled from loose wiring and bent metal. He looked into the sky and saw the other jet flying off into the distance. At that moment, he wasn't sure if it was retreating or getting the range to circle back for another attack.

Noah hurried over to Elly and placed the supplies in front of her. He gently soaked up the blood from her hair and told her to hold the towel in place. He cleaned it with peroxide carefully, as her expression showed her discomfort with the burning sensation. He tightly wrapped her head with the bandage several times and tied it over. The blood slowly soaked through.

"We can clean it again in a little while," Noah said as he stashed the rest of the supplies in a nearby corner that lacked debris. He placed a water bottle in her hand. "Drink up. You must stay hydrated."

"Thank you, Noah," Elly said, smiling. She slowly tilted the water bottle up and drank aggressively after being dehydrated for hours.

Noah returned the smile. He peered out again toward the monster, cluelessly looking into the sky for the third jet.

BANG!

The jet returned at sonic speed, rushing toward the monster. It fired two missiles, hitting the monster in its back. It roared with anger while descending to a simmer of pain. The monster bled, but not nearly enough to kill it. The jet shot into the sky, evading into sonic speed.

"I think this jet has a fighting chance," Noah said to Elly. "It landed some good shots already."

Elly smiled with tired eyes. She propped herself up in her seat. The jet returned for another pass. The monster looked frantically at the sky, trying to locate the jet. It sped toward the monster, aiming at its back.

The jet fired two more missiles, and they sped down toward their target. The monster threw its head back, looking into the sky, right at the jet. A beam shot out of its mouth again, absorbing the oncoming missiles. Unable to evade at its current speed, the jet flew into the beam. Noah swore it glowed for a second before exploding into a ball of fire. The monster returned to its seated position, letting out a tiresome groan, and tended to its wounds some more.

"That was the last one, wasn't it?" Elly asked.

Noah looked back at her, still in awe of the defeat he'd just witnessed. "It was. It's still alive."

Elly reached up to clear the hair from her face. Noah couldn't help but lock eyes with her out of concern and attraction. She looked up at him with her troubled expression.

"What do we do?" Elly asked.

"We need to get further away from it," Noah said nervously. He had fewer hopes for that plan working out. "You're in no condition to move anywhere, though."

Elly pushed off the wall, rising to her feet. Noah bolted over to help her. "That changes nothing. We need to go."

"Elly, you can't-"

"I can make it a few more blocks. We can hide up in Union Towers," Elly said, pointing down the street. "It's still standing high."

"Let's go," Noah said, throwing Elly's arm over his shoulder, lifting her to her feet. "I think we could get an impressive deal on a two-bedroom."

Noah walked carefully, half-carrying and half-walking Elly between debris and destroyed vehicles. He frequently looked up to see if they'd caught the monster's attention. With each block they passed, he felt slightly safer as the monster sat there, still. It shifted its body and often peered into the sky, like a giant puppy waiting for its next meal.

They approached the entrance of Union Towers and walked toward the stairs. They both gazed around before they climbed. It was a luxurious building, suited for people with much higher incomes. They both were guilty of staring at the building from a distance, longing to one day get the chance to live there, even if they knew it wouldn't happen.

Floor after floor, they were both excited to get the chance of being inside, even if the building lacked half of the windows, and part of the upper floors had walls blown out. They climbed and climbed, getting toward the fifteenth floor. Elly reached for the door handle when they approached the entrance in the stairwell.

"I think this is high enough," Elly said with labored breaths from her steep climb. "I want to see the entire city."

"Okay. Let's pick one," Noah said, pulling the door open. They walked through and stood at the end of the hallway. They looked at all the doors that had small decorations and expensive doormats. At the end of the hall was a ray of light from the last apartment. They could hear the wind echoing in the apartment they both knew was exposed to the outside from the damage. They walked down that way and looked inside.

There were still plates on the dinner table. Food scraps still sat with the utensils, and glasses held swills of pricey wine. The television flickered as it played the early morning news, with an enormous crack across the screen. The couch sat askew, with shattered glass piercing its fine leatherwork. The tall windows, now an open space, were shattered across the living space to the door.

Noah sat Elly on a safe part of the couch. They both looked out of the window and saw most of the city in wreckage. Noah walked over to the opening, gripping the steel support beam that once had once framed the tall windows in place. He saw everything—the city he'd inhabited for years—almost destroyed. The monster sat near the water, tending its wounds. The only other standing building was slowly collapsing, seven blocks away. He saw pieces break off of nearby buildings every few minutes.

"I always dreamed of looking out of this building in better circumstances. It's still beautiful to see,"

Elly said. Her voice grew softer with every word she spoke. Noah approached her and knelt in front of her.

"Let's get you cleaned up again," Noah said. He glanced at her bandage. It was soaked through and dripped down her ear. She had a dazed look in her eyes, but maintained a smile as she gazed out toward the city. She touched Noah's forearm.

"Thank you, Noah. It means a lot to me that I got to see this," Elly said.

"You're welcome. I'll be right back," Noah said.

Noah entered the bathroom and searched through the cabinets. He wrangled up some hand towels and a few tubes of Neosporin. He examined the hall closet and found a bottle of peroxide, and rushed over to Elly.

Noah froze. He looked down at Elly to see she was dead. The blood dripped down her ear to her neck. Her eyes were still open, gazing into the desecrated skyline. She leaned on the armrest, frozen in place. He dropped the materials and knelt to look into her eyes. They didn't move, even though he stared frantically, hoping to find life again.

Tears dripped down Noah's cheeks, and he sobbed uncontrollably. He felt alone for the first time since he'd first escaped his residence. Elly had been the only hope he'd felt for himself. He never believed he would leave the city. A faint humming came from the distance. Noah stood up and noticed it came from the sky.

He looked up to see a plane with a weird V-shape flying higher than he'd seen a plane rise. The monster rose to its feet, roaring into the air. It shot a beam from its mouth, but the plane was too high to be hit by the monster's assault. The beam lost its momentum below the altitude the plane flew at. The doors of the plane opened from the bottom, and Noah saw something fall out of it.

This is the one that'll kill it, he thought. He knew it had power, based on the size of it. It dropped slowly, but it was coming directly for the monster. Noah guessed it didn't intimidate the monster, since it had won all the other fights. Almost five hundred feet from the ground and the missile flew down faster. The monster stood its ground, roaring at it like it knew intimidation would stop it.

Two hundred feet. The missile ejected its shell, and fire shot out of the base. It flew rapidly toward the monster. Fifty feet. The monster jumped into the air, trying to strike the missile. It shot through the large opening the monster had between its arms. As if the plane was dropping a basketball, the monster made a perfect hoop to catch it. The missile struck the ground, and Noah saw a crater form. The monster hovered in the air for a few seconds while the blast reached its full power.

An entire block became a mound of dirt. Buildings collapsed into the ground, cars folded, and sidewalks sank into the subways. The monster flew toward Noah. It got as high as eighty feet into the air before landing at the base of Union Towers. Its head smashed into the first four floors. The building rocked and echoed, the sound of thousands of windows being shattered and raining down on the monster, further injuring it.

It raised its head to let out a whine and groaned in pain. Noah regained his footing and peered down, out of the exposed window, to see the monster. It had lost a chunk of its arm, had a severed foot, and badly burned skin. The monster looked up at Noah and they locked eyes. It was the first time that it knew it wasn't winning. The blast had knocked the fight right out of its body. Dark blue blood had drenched the building and dripped down the glass that held in place.

Part of the building cracked, and the floor slanted toward the window Noah stood near. He gripped onto it quickly. Looking back at the apartment, he saw Elly, now on the ground, slowly sliding toward him. Noah reached his hand out, trying to catch her as she got closer. He gripped her forearm so she wouldn't slide into the belly of the monster. He peered into her empty eyes, trying to focus on her innocence and beauty he'd indulged in briefly while she was alive.

The humming returned. Noah looked up and saw the doors open again on the plane. Out came another missile, headed right for the nearly defeated monster. It dropped faster and faster. The shell ejected from the body with a burst, and acceleration increased more and more. The monster roared. It was a unique tone Noah hadn't yet experienced; he heard the pain in its voice. Noah locked eyes with it again, roaring at Noah like it was asking for help. He froze.

It was responsible for Elly's death. It had decimated the city that Noah called home. It had made Noah feel lonelier than he ever had. Still, Noah felt remorse, like he was staring at his childhood pet, waiting to die in front of him. The missile struck the monster, burying it deep inside the building. Noah gripped tightly onto the support beam and Elly's arm. Then he felt the blast.

The entire building vibrated before crumbling down to the ground. Noah dropped and felt like he was falling for several minutes. He lost his grip on Elly almost immediately. He floated in the air while dust and smoke blinded him. He crashed down onto the wreckage, snapping his spine and shredding his limbs. His last moments of life were being showered by the now destroyed monster's blood. The rest of the building buried them both. The air would echo with the sound of the blast and collapse for several more minutes.

The plane flew off into the distance after dropping its final missile. The faint humming became a whisper, and then it was nothing at all. The dust cleared, and what remained of the offensive attack was a decapitated monster and not one standing building in the entire city. There were small sounds of cement falling or glass breaking, but a calm had settled over the defeated city.

The wind blew through the wreckage and carried no sounds of survivors, busy streets, or traffic. The city Noah had known forever, gone in a matter of less than a day. No one would dine out this evening. The commuters wouldn't be causing delays for anyone. The bars wouldn't host any crowds of coworkers enjoying a drink after work, or single people enjoying the nightlife that evening.

There was neither a yesterday nor a tomorrow to be experienced again. All was destroyed. All was quiet.

14

The Last Snowfall

THE SNOW HAD STARTED falling several miles back. Henry had his wipers on full speed, as the snow fell faster with each passing moment. The dimly lit street, with fewer streetlights in between one another, was becoming a black void except for the snowfall glowing in the headlights.

The evening radio circulated between Christmas music, weather reports, and static as Henry cycled between the frequencies in his range. He had traveled several hours that day, and he knew he was close to his destination from the GPS speaking to him. Cars passed him, but they grew further apart as Henry neared the end of his journey.

Henry turned on his phone that rested on the wireless charger mounted on the dashboard. He dialed his mother, Jen. It rang several times before connecting. Even though he heard her answer, she didn't respond right away. Syncing with the car radio, a loud blast of holiday music, noisy family members, and background noise, which sounded like a holiday movie, burst out through the speakers.

"Jesus," Henry said, spinning the volume dial down quickly.

"Hold on; it's Henry... Hello, sweetie. Are you here yet?" Jen asked excitedly.

"No, I still have a ways to go. Probably another forty minutes," Henry said. He slowly pulled his car to the side of the road.

"I know. I know," Jen said, speaking to family members in the background. It was always a pet peeve of Henry's. "Okay, Henry. Uncle Dave asked if you could pick up some more wine."

"Mom, I can barely see in front of the car. I'd rather just come straight home," Henry said, growing slightly more irritated.

"You know how much your uncle likes wine, though," Jen said.

"Well, since you put it that way...no," Henry said.

"No need to be snappy. If you pass by a liquor store, just stop," Jen said.

"That cheapskate better pay me back," Henry snapped.

"He will. I'll make sure he does. I love you, honey. Drive carefully."

He hung up almost immediately. Henry knew his mom could be a bit annoying after she'd had a glass or two, but she was probably starting her fourth, based on how she was slightly slurring her words. He was going to ask her if she needed anything while he was out, but she'd annoyed him enough that he wasn't stopping for Uncle Dave or her. He turned on his blinker and got back on the road.

The snow had picked up speed now, and Henry struggled to see in front of him. His wipers couldn't keep up with the white flakes that seemed like deep space travel rather than poor weather. The GPS stalled and lagged as he drove further.

"RECALCULATING. SIGNAL LOST."

Henry pulled his car over and shifted into park. He tilted the GPS with the hopes of it finding a signal— but it didn't. His phone struggled to find a signal simultaneously.

"Shit!" Henry exclaimed out of frustration. He grabbed his phone and stepped out of the car. He tightened his hood to cover his face from the heavy wind and intense chill in the air. He put his phone high in the air, but the service was stagnant. He moved all around and nearly fell into a ditch. He adjusted his stance and noticed a body in the snow.

"Hey, are you okay?" Henry asked loudly.

The wind was the only noise that escaped the dampening silence of the snow. There weren't any cars in either direction, and there hadn't been in quite a long time, which Henry had just noticed. He walked over to the body and realized why they didn't respond. The pool of blood surrounding it was enough to tell Henry they were dead.

"Oh, my God," Henry said, stumbling back in horror, almost losing his footing while navigating his steps in the deep snow. It was the first time he'd experienced something of this magnitude. A former high school friend was decapitated in a car accident when he was eighteen, but he only saw the bloody mess on the evening news. Several lacerations were evident across the body. Torn muscle and exposed bone made Henry believe there was an intense altercation with the killer.

Panicking, he returned to his car. Henry started the car and drove down the street quickly. Every house was as dark as the night he struggled to navigate. The streetlights offered slight illumination until he saw some house lights at the end of the street. He blared his horn while turning into the driveway. Henry stepped out of the car while still blaring the horn from outside of his car door.

"Hey! I need help! Please call 911!"

A silhouette stepped out of the front door. Henry could barely make out the figure, but slowly walked toward the house. Henry slipped. He flew forward, knocking his head on the pavement. Henry spotted the red splatter next to him while feeling intense pain in on the side of his head. Darkness overpowered the severe white storm.

Henry opened his eyes to find himself on a stranger's couch in front of a fireplace. His head throbbed, and he could feel a bandage tightly wrapped just above his eyebrow. He sat up slowly, trying to determine where he was and how long he'd been there. He heard footsteps immediately. Henry looked behind himself to see a lean older man coming to aid him.

"You need to keep your head down, son. You had a terrible fall. My wife, Rose, is making you some dinner as we speak," the man said with a smile across his face. Henry didn't know if it was the injury or not, but the man's smile was horrifying. "I'm Dennis. We will take great care of you."

"How long have I been here?" Henry asked. He shifted in his resting position to find himself in different clothes than when he'd arrived. His watch and cell phone were gone. "Where's my stuff?"

"Relax. Your clothes got soaked when you fell. They're in the dryer now, and your electronics are drying in a bowl of rice. Such a neat trick, if you ask me. I wish I were the guy who discovered that method," Dennis said. The smile was still eerie to Henry.

There was clattering a clattering in the kitchen. A shuffle of plates and appliances ringing briefly followed. Henry's vision adjusted to see a small, older woman coming toward Dennis and himself. She was also smiling, which appeared less disturbing than her husband's. Rose put the food tray down on the coffee table and sat at the edge of the couch to look at Henry.

She placed her hand on Henry's knee. A chill shot up his spine and made him quiver. It quickly overwhelmed Henry just how uncomfortable they were making him, despite being so polite.

"I'm Rose. It's so nice to meet you. I made some soup and some fresh bread for you. Feel free to stay as long as you like. We don't get many visitors, and it's been so long since we had to take care of anyone," Rose said.

Henry shifted again, getting more comfortable. He slowly sat up to face the food. Dennis put his hand on Henry's back as he sat upright. The chill came back once Henry felt Dennis's touch. He inspected the food and saw nothing suspicious. Henry didn't consider that Dennis and Rose were psychotic in any regard, but he couldn't shake the gut feeling that radiated through his body.

Get the hell out of here before it's too late, he thought. He dipped the spoon in the soup and brought it to his lips.

The warmth was euphoric. He hadn't tasted anything so good in a long time. His eyes lit up with each sip. Dennis chuckled.

"I've been married to her for almost sixty years, and it's the first time every time. Best soup on the planet, darling," Dennis said, gazing at Rose. She couldn't help but blush.

"You're too good to me, dear," Rose said.

Suddenly, their touch and smiles weren't as troubling. Henry indulged in the food and felt new life in his body. The throbbing in his head went down with the food. Each bite was the best food he'd ever eaten. The bowl was empty, and the bread vanished before Henry realized it. Rose's smile lit up again when she saw the plate bare before her.

"I guess I still got it, Dennis," Rose chuckled. "I'll get you some more..."

"Henry. My name is Henry," Henry said.

"Well, Henry, round two is coming right up!" Rose said. She smiled at Henry, and the feeling came back to his gut.

Just run out the door already!

Rose went to the kitchen and returned to the usual clatter of food prep. Henry noticed Dennis had sat beside him in a nearby chair and was staring like before. Henry broke eye contact to fight his gut feeling.

"So, Dennis, have you both lived here all of your lives?" Henry asked. "I don't normally come out here. Especially when the weather is so bad."

"This was close to our son when we were looking for homes. He needed a lot of attention, even as an adult," Dennis said.

"Does he still live around here?" Henry asked. The chill came back immediately.

Dennis's face went south quickly as an angry expression glared at Henry. There was hate behind the stare, and Henry couldn't break eye contact.

"Darling, could you give me a hand, please?" Rose asked from the kitchen.

Dennis looked away from Henry and smiled toward the kitchen. "Of course, my love."

Henry felt like he couldn't breathe from that glare. *Leave right now. Go while they're not looking!*

Henry looked around, trying to find the door. It stared back at him from the other side of the house. The ability to stand was still a challenge for him, but pushing off the couch was enough to get him started. He stood upright, but felt the weight of his injury force him back down. He tried a second time, peeking into the kitchen to see the old couple still busy with their cooking.

I have to find my phone! I need to talk to someone- The body!

Henry had completely forgotten about the body he'd found. The massive hit directly to his head surely made the experience slip his mind. He needed to get to a phone and call the police about it, and fast. Henry put one foot in front of the other, slowly shifting toward the kitchen entrance. Each step got slightly more manageable. He watched each foot swing in front of the other, stabilizing, trying to focus on making his way to the kitchen. He felt Dennis's hand again.

"Woah there, son, we need to get you back on the couch. You're not ready to be moving around just yet," Dennis said. He threw his arm around Henry and walked him back to the couch. Henry instantly felt relaxed when he felt the couch again.

I'm too comfortable here. Did they put something in my food?

"Listen, I appreciate you both helping me out, but I need to get in touch with someone. Can I please have my phone?" Henry asked.

"Your phone is still drying. I checked it a few minutes ago," Dennis said.

"May I please borrow yours?" Henry asked.

"I'm afraid not. I can be such a klutz in my old age! I dropped mine in the sink this afternoon. I was going to head to the electronic store to get a new one, but the storm ruined those plans. Luckily, my Rose is always with me, so I don't need to make any calls for a few days," Dennis said.

"I need to make a phone call. It's an emergency. Can you see if my phone is ready-" Henry said. Rose startled him when she appeared next to him with a tray of food.

"I can tell you're still hungry. I made a fresh batch of food," Rose said. Her smile was now as creepy as Dennis's.

They're blocking me in. I need to get out of here!

"I appreciate it, but I really need to call someone. I saw someone out in the snow, and they were bleeding. They could be dying or already dead.

Please," Henry said. Rose placed the tray down on the table and put her hand on Henry's shoulder.

"Nonsense. No one has been outside in hours. Your eyes were playing tricks on you. You had a nasty fall, and you are staying put until you are better. I will not be responsible for you hurting yourself," Rose said.

She dipped the spoon into the soup and reached up to feed Henry. "Now, eat up. You'll need it for strength."

Henry ate slowly. Each bite was as heavenly as the first batch. He swallowed a few more spoonfuls before looking up to see their piercing smiles again. Both sets of eyes were locked on him. Henry felt like their eyes could see through him.

Am I sweating? Can they notice? I need to charge for the door, get in my car, and keep on driving.

Henry put his spoon down, giving his smile and nod of approval once again. Rose didn't move at all. She kept on smiling at Henry. Henry noticed Dennis was doing the same.

"I'm so grateful for your hospitality, but I really need to use a phone. I can't have my family worrying," Henry said.

"Why don't you get some rest, and you can call first thing after breakfast tomorrow morning?" Rose asked.

"Please, I need to call-" Henry said. Dennis gripped his shoulder firmly. Henry jumped.

"I think you should get some rest. It would ease your nerves," Dennis said.

"You aren't listening to me. I need to make a phone call. It's urgent. I'm supposed to be somewhere tonight, and if I don't show up, I'm going to look like an asshole to my entire family," Henry shouted.

Dennis squeezed Henry's shoulder. "I'd appreciate it if you didn't talk like that in front of my wife. It's foul language."

"It's okay, dear. It's a critical situation, and I can understand his frustration," Rose said. Her smile was much more haunting now.

"Then you should let me make a call, and I can be on my way," Henry said.

Dennis and Rose didn't respond. They looked at each other, shrugging. Dennis stood up and walked into the kitchen. He brought back the phone, handing it to Henry.

"Thanks," Henry muttered. He dialed the number and waited for it to ring.

Adding to his series of misfortune, Henry reached his mom's voicemail. "Just my damn luck."

Henry clicked the phone off and placed it down on the coffee table. He looked up at Rose. She pushed the food tray closer to him. "Eat up, please. You'll need your strength. You can try calling again in a few minutes."

"I'll eat once I get in touch with someone. I need to make sure they know I'm all right," Henry said. He reached for his phone, but Dennis grabbed it first.

"You should eat first, son. It would make us feel better," Dennis said, sliding Henry's phone into his pocket. "You can have this back once you finish."

"Excuse me, please give my phone back. You have no right to take it," Henry said.

Dennis walked over to the bookshelf and placed Henry's phone on the middle shelf. He looked down at Henry, smiling. "Relax, son. It's right here where you can see it."

"Why do you keep calling me 'son'? I'm not your son. I hope you don't drive your kid this crazy," Henry said. He looked at Rose. Her eerie smile immediately turned to disgust. She stood and stepped back from Henry as if he'd turned into a swarm of insects. Dennis approached Henry with the same reaction Rose had.

"What the hell did you just say?"

"Do you drive your son crazy like this?" Henry asked.

Dennis glared over at Rose, sharing a furious expression. Rose approached the coffee table and flipped the food tray over, splashing soup across the living room. Henry sat back, scared, looking into their angry eyes.

"How dare you! After our hospitality, you should be a well-mannered young man. We don't deserve so much disrespect!" Rose shouted.

Dennis gripped Henry's bandage. Henry let out a groan of pain and looked Dennis in the eye. "You're hurting me!"

"You asked about our son. He was a lot like you. Ungrateful of our help, rude, selfish. We spent years helping him fix his mistakes, and not once did we ever get a thank you. We love our boy, but there's a line that kids shouldn't cross when it comes to how they treat their parents. He flew over that line like a fucking fighter jet!" Dennis yelled. He got right in Henry's face.

"He was beyond saving. Beyond redeeming himself for us, for his friends, and the society he thought he belonged in. I cut that useless boy's throat and let him bleed out in the dirt. I was hoping the snow would cover him and deal with him later but, just my luck, the second worse asshole on the planet finds him and stumbles onto my yard!"

Dennis slammed Henry's head back. He stormed off into the kitchen and grabbed a large kitchen knife. Henry tried to stand, but Rose held him down.

"Now you've done it, boy," Rose whispered. "Now you've set him off."

Henry struggled from Rose's grip, but she dug her nails into his wound. Blood trickled down from his bandage, and he shrieked in pain. He pushed at her but couldn't break free. Dennis approached Henry quickly and slashed his chest. Rose released him, and Dennis threw Henry onto the coffee table. Henry fell back and slammed down on the living room floor. He tried crawling to the door.

"You're just like him. Wasting all of my time for your own needs," Dennis said as he swung the knife down into Henry's back. Henry shrieked again.

"Please stop!" Henry yelled.

Dennis reached down and flipped Henry over to face him. Dennis sat on Henry's chest and swung the knife down into Henry's shoulder. Dennis pulled it out and swung it down again into his chest. Blood shot out of Henry's mouth.

"I think I'll leave you right next to my son!" Dennis yelled, raising the knife above his head.

"Wait, please wait-" Henry said while choking on his blood.

Dennis swung the knife into Henry's forehead, killing him instantly. Rose shrieked when she saw Henry go limp.

"Dennis, you already made a mess of the rug earlier. It's going to take forever to get all that blood out!" Rose yelled.

"Relax, Rose. I'll clean up the blood. Just give me time to get rid of him," Dennis said.

"At least put him in a tarp first. I don't need you dragging more blood around," Rose said.

Rose scooped up the last of the food and walked into the kitchen to empty it all into the sink. Dennis grabbed a tarp from the porch and spread it across the floor. He pushed Henry's body onto it and rolled him tightly. He wrapped the tarp with Henry's fresh corpse inside.

"No sense of breaking my back for him. I'll let the snow bury him and deal with him when it gets warmer," Dennis said. "Is that okay with you, Rose?"

"Fine, but turn out the living room lamp. I don't need you killing anyone else this evening. Give it a day or two. I'm stressed by Junior giving me all that grief," Rose said.

"I didn't plan on this little prick coming in tonight, but that's life," Dennis said. "How about a movie in the bedroom?"

"That sounds lovely, dear. Once we finish up," Rose said. She handed him some rags and the rug cleaner.

Dennis walked over and wrapped his arms around Rose, kissing her deeply. He smiled at her and bent down to clean up the blood.

15

Heat Form

I AM A PART of you now. I am your body now.

"No, get out of my head. Get out of my body!"

We are one, Heather. Show me who to feed on, and I'll show you a new, better form.

The shotgun cocks as Heather pumps a shell into the barrel. An extension, similar to an arm but with decrepit skin and muscle, locks the barrel before bending it down toward the trigger. It pulls the gun from Heather's firm grip and launches it across the room.

We may share a body, but my strength is beyond yours. Allow me to be your equal, and we can have greatness together.

Heather screams as her back contorts against her will. Her spine extends beyond what her vertebrae allow, and she drops to her knees. Her bra strap snaps, and the stitching in her shirt tears, exposing her shoulders and letting her shirt fall to her breasts.

We are one. One and only one.

Heather shoots awake, flying out of bed as if she were launched by force. She rushes to the bathroom and stares at her sweat-drenched face in the mirror. She collects her composure after her haunting nightmare.

One and only one!

Heather returns to her room and cranks down the air conditioner to sixty degrees. She stands near it for several seconds before returning to bed. As she turns to get comfortable on her side, a tremendous growth on her back flattens to its normal state. Heather falls back asleep, and the growth within her does, too.

DENNIS ADMIRES HIMSELF IN the mirror while combing his hair into his signature pompadour. He flicks his comb against the thick pomade, humming a song that he thinks was written for him. While he pulls the comb from the thick product coating his hair, his phone vibrates on the dresser. He taps the speaker button so he can continue his daily ritual.

"Yo, bro," Dennis said.

It is the only greeting he has ever said to his best friend, Clark. A self-absorbed man like Dennis, Clark is always picking up women, treating them poorly, and bragging to Dennis about his usual womanizing antics. It wasn't until Clark slept with a significant number of women that Dennis picked up the habit of routinely disrespecting his sexual partners. They'd once slept with the same woman in one day and went on to ridicule her for being promiscuous.

"So, are you doing this or not? I need an answer," Clark said.

"The webcam thing? I don't know, dude. Don't get me wrong, my dick is something to be admired, but I don't think I need my friends seeing it."

"Bro, everyone thinks you're a god for snatching up Heather. Why not reap the benefits of being the one who fucks her, live on camera?" Clark said in excitement. He had been pushing Dennis about his latest plan for several days now.

Even Dennis was skeptical of Clark's new plan of archiving their sexual escapades for some crappy porn site, but their reputation would soar amongst their group of friends.

"Do I need to? I can go the rest of my life missing out on this. Especially since I'm going to hear Keith say 'Bro, I jerked it to your video. Not to you, because I'm no homo, but she was so hot, bro.' I told you, I can get you guys nudes before the weekend is over."

"Nudes are too 2010!" Clark exclaimed. "I want to see how that girl takes that dick."

"I'll think about it, Clark. I have to go. I'll call you once Heather and I get to the beach house."

"Remember, bro, there could be some money in it for us," Clark said. "If we give them enough business, we get a cut of the royalties."

"Talk to you later, bro."

Dennis clicked the phone off. He dropped his comb on the dresser and made his way to a tall mirror to admire his attire. His designer pants and polo, that both cost more than most people spend on round trip flights, were looking sharp on his toned physique. He gave himself a smile and a confident nod before grabbing his duffel bag, exiting his apartment to hop into his convertible, and speeding down the road.

Heather packed the remainder of essentials in her weekend bag. She placed it on her couch and grabbed a glass from the cabinet. She filled it with cold water from the faucet and drank it down. She filled a second glass and swallowed it down.

You'll have to expose me sooner or later.

"I'm going to stall as long as I can." Heather felt even crazier talking to a voice inside her head, let alone talking to a growth living inside her own body. She'd only be crazier to tell someone the truth, she thought.

I'm looking forward to when I get out.

"Plenty of air conditioner to kill your excitement."

If you don't let me out, I'll force myself out.

"Go ahead. Good luck living for very long without a host."

The doorbell interrupted Heather's intimate conversation. She walked over to pull the door open, revealing Dennis standing before her.

"Hey, you," Dennis said, smiling and reaching in to kiss Heather. "Ready?"

"Hey. Yeah, let's go."

Dennis grabbed Heather's bag and walked out. Heather closed and locked the door behind her. Dennis wrapped his hand around her waist as Heather smiled up at him.

"I hope you're ready for the weekend I have planned," Dennis said.

"I've been looking forward to it all week." Heather smiled as she opened her door and climbed into the car. Dennis got in on his side and sped down the road. They made their way to the highway.

Dennis flew through the light traffic. Between Heather and himself, they switched back and forth, choosing music that blasted from the speakers. They held hands, and Dennis took a few gulps from his twenty-ounce energy drink.

"What time are we getting there?" Heather asked.

"We have another two hours ahead of us," Dennis said. "Trust me. It'll be worth the wait. My dad used to take us here every summer as kids. Not even thirty feet from the water."

"I can't wait to feel that water on my toes." Heather cranked the air conditioner up and adjusted in her seat. Dennis glared at her for dialing the air up.

"Babe, I'm going to freeze to death. It's not even that hot out."

"Sorry, my AC died last night. I think I'm just more sensitive to the heat after sweating all night."

Dennis gave her an irritated look, and she smiled at him before leaning in to kiss him on the cheek. He looked at his phone as it vibrated from a text. It was Clark. He tapped it open when Heather was distracted by her phone again.

'Please take my advice and hit record. Big paycheck coming our way!'

Dennis rolled his eyes and clicked his text away and returned his phone to the dashboard. He dialed the AC down a few degrees. Heather hadn't noticed while she played with her phone.

She flicked through her social media, smiling at the occasionally humorous post or lifestyle page she found to be helpful for her self-care routine. She felt a bump on her back, expanding slightly, and ignored it for a few seconds. When it started to extend further, she gasped and cranked the air up.

Don't bury me, or I'll make sure your family buries you!

"Hey, can you pull off at the next rest station, please? I need to use the bathroom!" Heather exclaimed, making it sound much more severe to Dennis than he thought was necessary. Dennis looked at her with a confused expression.

"Babe, we're going to be late, and that doesn't even factor in the traffic."

Dennis was stern with his response. He had timed everything perfectly. So ideally, in fact, that he was expecting to be in bed with Heather in precisely eight hours as he said it.

"We need to stick to our planned arrival time."

"Please, I promise I'll be quick," Heather said, trying not to sound as desperate as she felt.

Dennis couldn't help but roll his eyes as he signaled into the right lane and swung into the rest stop. He threw the car into park and gave Heather a sarcastic pout.

"Be quick," Dennis said. "Don't come back to the car without getting me a soda."

"Candy, too," Heather said, leaning in to kiss him on the cheek.

Heather walked into the building to find a market filled with snacks and travel-sized goods. She grabbed several snacks and briefly browsed the travel goods. She saw instant cold packs hanging from the shelf as if they were meant for her. She grabbed two, purchased everything, and rushed into a bathroom stall. She removed the packs from the packaging and slid them underneath her bra strap, near the clasp. She adjusted and then pulled her shirt back down.

"That should hold you over," Heather said quietly to herself.

They'll run out, just like your will to defeat me.

"It hasn't yet. Sleep tight."

Heather grabbed her purse and made her way out to the car. She dropped down into her seat, giving Dennis the candy and soda she'd got for him. She closed the door, and Dennis returned to the highway, flying through traffic to make up for the time she'd taken off their trip while postponing her impending doom.

IT WAS EVENING WHEN Dennis and Heather pulled into the driveway of the beach house. They emerged from their car seats. Heather stretched her arms while Dennis let out a loud groan following his stretch.

"Goddamn, that drive took way longer than it needed to," Dennis complained. "Between that accident on the highway and your bathroom stops, it cost us another two hours."

Heather looked at him with sympathetic eyes while she thought that he was a baby about the whole situation.

"We're here now. Let's make the best of it." Heather walked over to Dennis and kissed him before walking toward the front door. "I can't wait to shower."

"My thoughts exactly."

Dennis grabbed their bags from the trunk and walked into the house behind Heather. The sunset glowed amber against the windows overlooking the water. The faint rhythmic sound of water lapping the shore could be heard in the living room where Dennis briefly dropped Heather's bag.

Heather walked into the kitchen, looking out at the view before searching the fridge. She grabbed a water bottle and drank it down. Dennis walked toward the bedroom with their bags firmly grasped in his hands.

"What are we doing about food?" Heather asked.

"There are menus in the top drawer of the island. Pick something out. I'm gonna use the bathroom. Feel free to shower in the hallway bathroom."

"Sounds good, babe. I'll wait until you're done. The food will take a little while, anyway." Heather approached her purse and bent over to search through it. Dennis paused to gaze at Heather's visible cleavage while she inspected the items in her purse. He took a deep breath and entered the bedroom, closing the door. He tossed his bag on the bed after pulling his laptop out and placing it on the desk. He turned it on and loaded the webcam to see the entire room on the screen.

"Now, let's see how to do this," Dennis said to himself. He pulled the laptop closer to the edge of the desk, eliminating the dead space of the room on the screen, and making the center of the screen focus on the bed.

"Perfect."

He closed the laptop. He opened his phone to Clark's conversation.

'I'll do it.'

Not even ten seconds went by before Clark responded.

'You won't regret it, bro. Tell me when you're ready. I want to watch the entire thing.'

Dennis immediately felt lingering guilt in his gut, but he knew the money would be worth it. As long as Heather didn't discover what he was up to, it wouldn't be a problem. Just another sweet pair of tits online, he thought. He entered the bathroom and turned the shower on, ready to cleanse his body and clear his mind for his degrading plan.

DENNIS AND HEATHER SAT down to dinner. Her timing between ordering the food, taking a lengthy shower that didn't conflict with her internal problem, and dressing as the food arrived, impressed her and Dennis equally. They looked across the table, eyeing the vast options of Mexican, Greek, and Italian dishes. Dennis, confused, looked up at Heather.

"Quite the choices, Heather. Couldn't settle on one?"

"Mexican is pretty filling. You like Greek food, and I was craving some pasta."

Heather started serving right away, and Dennis served right after her. Some conversation followed their bites while planning the rest of their weekend.

"So, I was thinking of doing the beach tomorrow, and a few nearby restaurants. Tonight, we just stay indoors and do something a bit more intimate," Dennis said, smiling and trying to swallow his food.

"Well, that sounds good to me. Glad I packed for all of those occasions." Heather slurped her food, staring at Dennis while doing it.

"Don't torture me, please," Dennis whimpered, making Heather laugh.

"So, this is your dad's house? How long have you owned it?" Heather asked.

"He inherited it from my grandfather. When I was about seven, my grandfather became very ill and-"

Heather suddenly had a hard time hearing Dennis. His voice was muffled, as if he were speaking to her behind a wall. Dennis wasn't aware that he sounded faint to Heather. He kept on talking, unaware of Heather's struggle.

He doesn't know that you can't hear him. You can hear me, though, loud and clear. Pretty soon, everyone will be able to hear me. Pretty soon, the only thing you'll be able to hear is me.

"STOP!" Heather shot up from her seat, standing and dropping her silverware. She began to sweat. She wiped her brow, noticing the sweat and bulging sensation in her back.

"I'm sorry. I need to use the bathroom. I'm so sorry."

"No, it's okay. Take all the time you need," Dennis said.

Heather entered the bathroom and turned on the cold water. She ran her hands underneath the water and dabbed it on her face and forehead. She waited until she felt cooled down. She stopped the water and sat on the sink for a few moments.

"I won't let you win. I have enough help to bury you this weekend."

The beach for an entire day is enough for me to cut through your flesh and his. You will both be dead by Monday.

"Fuck you. When you do get out, I'll make sure you're out of my body for good."

A loud snap caused Heather to fall to the ground. Gripping her hand, she looked down at it, revealing several fingers bent backward.

I can't kill you, but I can make this very painful for you. I want him. Give me him, and this will all be over.

"As I said, fuck you."

Heather exited the room, walking back toward the table where Dennis waited patiently. She passed the bedroom and noticed the large cooler. She walked in and opened up a cold water bottle. She drank it down immediately, and while looking across the room, the computer screen caught her eye. She walked over to the laptop, revealing a large button that read "Record her!" on a site called Make Her Amateur.

"Make her amateur?" Heather said, annoyed and curious for more details.

She clicked around the page, fearing the worst of her companion in the next room. She couldn't believe he could be convinced to do something like this. She paced the room, back and forth, thinking of how to bring this up to him. A smile came across her face when she figured it out. She rushed over to her bag and began pulling out clothing.

Dennis was now concerned that Heather had been in the bathroom for so long. Thirty minutes or more went by, and he checked his watch to be sure.

"Heather, you okay in there?" He worried more about the lack of sex rather than if she was hurt or troubled in some way. Still, it was bothersome, to say the least.

"Yeah, I'll be right out. Sorry for the wait."

Heather stepped into sight, and Dennis dropped his utensils. He couldn't believe what Heather was wearing. Heather's body was decorated by a tight, black lace, one-piece. Her sleeves had a detailed design while her large breasts bulged from the low-cut opening in the front. She turned to reveal her back, exposing the cheeky bottoms that fit like underwear while her entire back was covered with fabric, stitched with a detailed design similar to the sleeves.

"You said you wanted tonight to be intimate," Heather said, brushing the hair from her face while smiling at Dennis.

"Uh... yes. Yes, that's right." "Well, come in here then."

Heather walked back into the bedroom. She sat on the bed, waiting for Dennis. She avoided looking at the laptop to make Dennis think she wasn't aware of it. Dennis rushed in, nearly out of breath. He smiled at her.

"Sorry for keeping you waiting," Heather said. "I figured maybe this would make it up to you."

"Th... thank you."

Heather chuckled. "Am I making you nervous?"

"Yes. You look so good." Dennis pulled his shirt over his shoulders, throwing it to the ground. He approached Heather quickly. She pushed against his chest to casually resist.

"Why don't you put music on to set the mood?"

"Right, good idea."

Dennis walked over to the laptop, quickly browsing his playlist for some appropriate music. He hit play and waited for Heather's response.

"That should do the trick."

He turned back to the laptop, carefully opening the website he thought was outside of Heather's knowledge. He clicked the "Record her!" button and walked over to Heather. He started unbuttoning his pants, but Heather stopped him.

"Use your tongue first," Heather said. "Do a good job, and I'll do anything you ask."

"Okay."

Dennis dropped to the floor, kneeling in front of Heather's legs. Spreading her open, he gently teased her while Heather couldn't help but moan and grip the sheets. She wasn't expecting her plan to work, let alone be pleasured this well by Dennis. It was a first to see him put in this much effort for her own libido. She was overwhelmed by the intensity of every move Dennis made.

He licked her in just the right spot, while stimulating her with multiple fingers. Each moan was louder than the next. Heather wasn't sure if she was ripping the sheets or pulling them off of the bed. The intensity wasn't thought out from the start. She could feel herself heating up, not worrying about the secret inside of her bursting out, but rather a natural reaction to burst out instead.

Several minutes went by and Dennis didn't stop for air. He continued on, using his tongue to please Heather more and more. She moaned out, occasionally shouting out a vulgarity or two while tugging more at his hair or the sheets. Sweat built up under her back. She was now conscious of the risk of sweating, but she knew something bigger was happening. Heather arched her back, losing her breath entirely.

She pulled at Dennis aggressively, unable to control herself. She yelled, riding out the biggest orgasm she'd had in years. Moaning, unable to be discreet for the video, and lacking concern anyway, she quivered until her body calmed down. She caught her breath and let go of her firm grip on Dennis.

Dennis sat up. "I could tell you enjoyed that."

"Yes, very much."

"What now? What can I do for you now?"

I can smell his blood.

"Take him," Heather said. "Take him now."

"What did you say? Take who?" Dennis asked.

I won't go easy on him. I need to feed.

"Take him... now!" Heather shouted, kicking Dennis in the gut.

He stumbled back. Dennis stood up angrily, looking back at Heather to yell at her. He instead grew horrified as her body contorted. Her back arched forward and two large spider-leg like extensions emerged from behind Heather.

Two large legs shot down to the ground, pushing Heather's feet off of the ground. Heather's body went limp as the growing limbs emerged more. Four more limbs extended out, revealing themselves as they pointed toward Dennis. Each limb was drenched in a slimy, red liquid that shimmered like glossy lacquer.

"Heather, what the fuck are you doing!?" Dennis yelled.

Heather's eyes locked on Dennis. She opened her mouth, revealing a tongue that had smaller spider-like extensions growing from it. She gripped the tongue firmly, pulling at it intensely. As Heather pulled, the being inside of her started to erupt from her throat. Heather gagged aggressively as it poured out of her mouth further and further. The extensions from her back retreated as she pulled at the distorted tongue, further and further, until she gasped for air.

She dropped back to her feet, trying to maintain her balance. The being—now outside of Heather's body—dropped to the floor in a pile of slimy flesh. Heather fell to her knees, weakened and exhausted.

"Heather, what the hell is that?"

"Did you seriously think you were going to fuck me and record it for the world to see?"

"Is that really what you're thinking about right-"

The mass of flesh shot out toward Dennis, sliding a tentacle down his throat. Dennis pulled at it while trying to breathe, but it overpowered him, sliding deeper down his throat. Dennis gagged, dripping saliva down the tentacle. His body swung back as the last bit of the fleshy mass slid down his throat, accepting his body as a new host. Heather gazed up at Dennis, motionless, frozen in place.

"Take him already!"

This body is undesirable.

"What? You were in mine for weeks. It's new, you can have him. Go on!"

I reject this body. However, I do need to eat.

"Who is that? Who's talking?" Dennis shrieked. "What's inside of me?"

"The same thing that was inside of me." Heather walked closer to Dennis, who now started to cry. "Let's see how you handle it."

With a loud snap, Dennis contorted inward. His back rotated in a semi-circle as the being sucked most of his flesh inward, feeding on his blood and intestines. His skin sagged like an obese man suddenly dropping hundreds of pounds. The mass on Dennis's body reduced and, and the being stood out from the rib cage that hosted it. Dennis folded forward as the snapping of his shattering bones failed to fold him upright.

His legs buckled and, and he dropped to the floor like a pile of bones inside a sagging bag of skin. Blood dripped from his eyes and nose. Saliva oozed out of his mouth like a leaky pipe.

Hardly worthy of my presence. It feels good to be rejuvenated!

"Let's see how long he can keep you alive," Heather yelled, running toward the door.

Heather rushed outside and slammed the door shut. She ran toward the car, unaware of how little her attire covered her from the outside world. She clicked the unlock button several times and hopped into the driver's seat. She started the car and peeled out of the driveway—speeding down the road—flying onto the highway.

She looked in the rearview mirror, illogically feeling that she was being followed. After several seconds, she burst into hysterical laughter. Not only was she free of the being that she'd hosted for weeks, but she was free of a man who was about to ruin her reputation for the entire world.

As she put miles of distance between her and that house, she realized that the entire encounter was captured online. Did someone know who she was? Did Dennis have friends who were watching or planned the whole thing? It wasn't much concern right now, as she pulled into a gas station to refuel her car. She stopped at a pump and exited the car. She emerged to realize that not only did she not have her wallet, but she was also in very revealing lingerie.

"Well damn, someone forgot to put her robe on," a man yelled from the nearby gas pump. "Damn, baby, that body is crazy."

Heather grew angry. Still, she knew this was a great opportunity for her. Heather walked over to the man, smiling.

"You like it?"

"I sure do. You are sexy."

"Well, my boyfriend couldn't handle it. Didn't even give me gas money before kicking me out."

"Damn fool if you ask me," the man said, shaking his head while staring at Heather.

"Tell you what, why don't you bring me back to his beach house? I'll make a feast out of you before the end of the night." Heather rubbed his chest while eyeing his convertible. "You can drive. Besides, maybe you'll see another top down."

"I'd love that. But what about your boyfriend? Won't he be at this beach house?"

"I'm sure he's worn out. I'll sneak you in, anyway." Heather smiled, looking right at the man. "Are you in?"

"Let's go." The man finished pumping his gas and opened the door for Heather. He got in the driver's side and turned onto the highway. They drove toward the beach house that had plenty more horrors waiting inside. Enough to please everyone until sunrise.

16

I Saw Her Floating

Haley walked down the long hallway toward her therapist's office. The agonizing wait, talking to the dreary receptionist, and finally opening the door to see the couch she's spent countless hours on still drained her energy to keep going.

"Good afternoon, Haley. How are you today?" Franklin asked.

Franklin had first met Haley two years ago, and spent the majority of that time listening to the troubled past Haley had endured. It wasn't until Hayley's sister, Alicia, commit suicide that Haley took a turn for the worst. Haley got comfortable on the couch. She liked to stare straight at the wall, regardless of if it ruined her posture. She stared intensely, unable to find the words to say next.

"I had a very vivid dream two nights ago, and I'm having a hard time processing it," Haley said.

"What sort of dream?" Franklin asked. "I saw Alicia again," Haley said.

"It's going to be a common occurrence that you see Alicia. She is in the center of your thoughts most of the time," Franklin said.

Haley paused because she couldn't explain the dream to him. It was the first time she'd seen Alicia in a bizarre state. All of her dreams usually reflected a memory with of Alicia, or seeing her somewhere casual casual, like the mall or grocery store. This dream, the one from last night, brought new insight to Haley.

"I think Alicia regretted committing suicide at the last minute," Haley said.

"I see. What brings you to that conclusion?" Franklin asked.

"Maybe it's best if I tell you what happened in the dream," Haley said.

"Please proceed," Franklin said.

HALEY WOKE TO FIND herself standing outside of her childhood home. Haley and Alicia moved from there when they were teenagers. It was nighttime, and the streetlights were dimmed to a soft glow, similar to a small bedroom lamp. The streets were empty, not. Not a single person was outside. Haley assumed it was the middle of the night, that it was a memory repeating itself in her head, and Alicia would emerge from behind the bushes, revealing that she'd lost another game of hide-and-go-seek.

Haley spotted a faint glow above the ranch-style house, and it intensified before it formed the shape of a human being. The person floated about fifteen feet above the house. It was the only motion in Haley's sight. People, cars, pets, or anything else to distract her hadn't caught her attention. It took Haley several moments to realize that the mysterious figure was Alicia, floating above the house. Haley stepped closer to Alicia. She didn't have a clue what to say or do.

"Alicia, is that you?" Haley asked.

"Hello, Haley. I've missed you," Alicia said.

Alicia's glow was fairly dim, but it started to pulse. Haley thought she heard Alicia whisper to herself, but she didn't make anything of it.

"I've missed you, too, Alicia. What made you think this was the best decision?" Haley asked.

"Ending my life, taking the path I took, suited the world accurately," Alicia said.

"That's not true at all, and you know it, Alicia," Haley said. "Seeing you in a casket was the hardest moment of my life."

"Waking every day, deciding to push on again after the previous was nothing short of misery, became the hardest moment of my life. I did what needed to be done," Alicia said.

The glowing around Alicia intensified. Alicia let out a faint whimper of pain. Barely audible to Haley, she passed it off. She stepped closer to the house and looked around the yard. Alicia's glow pulsed faster. Hearing another whimper, Haley knew the glowing was affecting Alicia.

"Is the light hurting you?" Haley asked.

"Nothing can hurt me anymore, sister," Alicia said.

"Why here? Why did you come to this house and not the home we live in now? The home I live in now, I should say," Haley said.

She looked on at Alicia above the house as the pulsing slowed to a steady glow. The brightness hardly made Haley squint, despite it dwarfing the streetlight's capabilities.

"It's where the thoughts began. I never felt like someone who belonged to my family, to my friends, or to the world. I knew one day I would tread along as an adult, trying to find a way to make life enjoyable, when I always felt it was a chore to get up and go on for another day. I made a promise to myself that one day I would find the courage to be stronger than my urge to survive my misery and commit to ending it all when the time was right," Alicia said.

"How could you possibly know the time was right to die?" Haley asked.

"When I woke up and knew I didn't want to live anymore," Alicia said. The glowing intensified, and Alicia yelled out. "It hurts so much, Haley."

Haley stepped closer, trying to look on. To her, it compared to staring directly into a headlight, yet she wanted to get to Alicia. She stepped forward again, but the glow around Alicia lit up the entire street. Alicia let out a scream that echoed down the road. Haley held her ears as the scream pierced her head like shards of glass. She stepped back, and the light dimmed down. Alicia took several deep breaths, and the pain subsided.

"I didn't realize I was doing that. I'm sorry," Haley said. "How can I help you, Alicia?"

"You can't help me. I'm gone, Haley," Alicia said.

"Then why are you here now?" Haley asked.

Alicia didn't answer as she hovered silently, staring into the sky. Haley could see tears dripping down her cheeks. Haley guessed her arms were weighed down by this forceful light because she made no effort to wipe her face. Alicia's gaze looked on into the night.

"I don't want to be dead anymore," Alicia whispered.

"What did you say?" Haley asked.

"I don't want to be dead anymore!" Alicia yelled.

The words left her lips, and the glow exploded across the sky. Haley yelled out from the blinding intensity. Alicia's scream echoed for miles. Tears poured out of her eyes like a fountain had blown a valve and erupted. Between covering her eyes and her ears, Haley felt as overwhelmed as Alicia seemed.

"I miss it all. I miss talking to you until the early hours of the morning, seeing my friends, talking to Mom and Dad. I want it all back," Alicia cried.

"You just said you didn't want to live anymore. You're confusing me, Alicia. I don't know what to do," Haley said as tears fell from her face.

She wept as much as Alicia as she saw her struggle with a decision she couldn't reverse.

"I wanted it every day for as long as I can remember. Now, after everything, it hurts more here. I'd bring back my worst day on Earth over any day here," Alicia said. "I can't stop the burning. I can't stop the pain I wanted to escape."

"What can I do, sister?" Haley asked. "Tell me, and I'll do it."

The glowing stopped and Haley stared up at Alicia. The silence, too intense for Haley, caused a stillness she hadn't known for quite a long time. There wasn't any indication that Alicia was suffering since the tears and screaming had halted. Still floating above the house, Alicia was motionless. Haley stepped toward the house slowly. With each small step, she kept her focus on Alicia, making sure not to trigger the painful glow around her late sister.

One of the bedroom lights burst brightly. As if a truck were parked in the room, flashing its high beams to Haley outside, the. The light was intense briefly until it dimmed to the usual glow someone would see if they gazed into a lit room from the darkness outside. Two silhouettes stood close to each other in the bedroom. Haley knew it was Alicia and herself when she heard their laughter. They stared at one another, giggling, while present Haley looked up at her possibly unconscious sister.

"What are the odds we get each other the same thing?" Haley laughed.

"I don't know, but I'm borrowing that this weekend. It's adorable," Alicia laughed.

They exploded in laughter as the light faded to nothing, and the two disappeared into the darkness of the house. Haley smiled slightly, remembering that moment and still being amused by the exchange. Another light turned on in the house. Haley sat at her desk, studying. She could hear the conversation like it was right beside her.

"Come on, let's go out. You can finish your homework tomorrow," Alicia said from outside the door.

Haley sighed, throwing her pen across her desk. "I told you, the test is tomorrow. I can't go out.

Can't you find something else to do?" Haley asked, composing herself before returning to her work.

"Yeah, I can. Sorry to bother you," Alicia said. She walked away from Haley's bedroom door and walked into her room, which illuminated. She approached her dresser and dug through the top drawer. She approached the window, becoming a silhouette in front of Haley. She raised her left arm to her eye level. In her right hand, Alicia held a razor and slowly moved it toward her left arm.

"No, no. Please, don't Alicia," Haley said from outside. "Please."

Alicia dragged the razor across the inside of her forearm quickly. Blood rushed down her arm and dripped to the tips of her fingers. She let out a sigh and went to make a second swipe. A third followed. A fourth soon after. Several drops were visible against the white curtains that blocked Haley's clear view of Alicia.

She knew it was bloodier than she could see. Alicia stood up and walked back to the dresser, putting the blade back and exiting her room. Both rooms went black. Haley stepped back, staring up at Alicia, still floating above the house. Haley sobbed as Alicia remained silent.

"Do you blame me, Alicia?" Haley asked. "Am I the cause of this?"

The light pulsated around Alicia's body. She was still quiet and motionless.

"Please, Alicia. If I caused this, I need you to tell me," Haley said as tears poured down her face. She buried her head in her hands and dropped to her knees.

Haley let the sadness overwhelm her for several seconds. She looked up at her floating sister. "Say something. Please!"

"You made it easier," Alicia whispered.

"What did you say?" Haley asked.

The lights inside the house exploded. The brightness illuminated the street. Haley fell backward from the sudden intensity. She tried to peer into the house, but the slightest glance made her eyes seal shut. She could see Alicia's silhouette reaching her wrists up again. This time, a large knife dragged across her wrist like a bow against a violin. Each slice sprayed the white curtain dark red.

Alicia swiped again and again until the silhouette faded in into the soaked darkness. The lights went black, and Haley was swallowed by the silence again.

She heard herself breathing, as if it were amplified for the entire neighborhood. A faint humming echoed, and Alicia moved for the first time in quite some time. Alicia's limbs extended as far as they could without separating from her body. She let out a blood-curdling scream and was consumed by the light again.

Her body glowed from the inside. The blacks of her eyes were brighter than the whites, and her ears, nose, and mouth became rays shooting into the air like lasers. The humming intensified. Haley could only translate one thing within from Alicia's screams.

"Bring me back. I don't want to be dead anymore," Alicia yelled.

The humming rang loud like a siren. Haley covered her ears, but it couldn't block the screams Alicia released.

"God, it hurts everywhere. Help me, Haley," Alicia screamed. Her body dematerialized as the light brightened. "I'm sorry! Make it stop! I don't want this anymore!"

"I don't know what to do!" Haley screamed. "I'm sorry! I'm so sorry!"

"Save me, please!" Alicia screamed.

She closed her eyes as they filled with the glow. Haley shielded her eyes. The humming rattled the windows, shattering them and blowing glass at Haley. She fell backward as shards ripped into her. She looked again and Alicia was nothing but an intense beam. It glowed for several more seconds before exploding in every direction. The sky lit up brighter than the daylight could offer. The night was momentarily gone and then suddenly back.

Haley stood up and pulled out the more massive shards of glass from her arm and stomach as blood dripped freely. She let out a moan as she pulled small pieces from her chest and abdomen. She dropped the glass and looked at the house. The boarded windows and the house were in irreparable condition, transformed from the beauty it had offered in her youth. Alicia was gone, and the house was quiet. The only light was from the streetlights nearby. One of them slowly burnt out.

"I'm sorry, Alicia," Haley said.

Two more streetlights burnt out.

"I'm so sorry," Haley said.

Three more streetlights faded to black.

"Please forgive me," Haley said.

The last streetlight welcomed the darkness.

HALEY ADJUSTED HERSELF IN the chair. She looked up at Franklin.

"It was as vivid as it sounds," Haley said.

"Haley, do you blame yourself?" Franklin asked.

"I don't know if it was my mind telling me what Alicia was saying, or if that was some sort of connection to her, but-" Haley said. Franklin raised his hand to interrupt her.

"Do you blame yourself for Alicia's death?" Franklin asked.

Haley didn't speak. After her dream, she'd never considered the thought. It wasn't clear to her if Alicia blamed her or not. She recalled the dream, the house, the silence, all of it. Haley remembered so many memories in that house and the happiness Alicia and her she shared there.

She remembered Alicia's slow degradation, and the long sleeve shirts to cover her cuts, despite the summer heat. She remembered Alicia screaming. She looked back at Franklin.

"No, I don't," Haley said. She put her head down.

"It was unfortunate that she couldn't find solace in talking about her problems. I want to reassure you that no matter what you could've done, this was her decision," Franklin said.

Haley looked up at the door. She looked down the hallway, staring at the wall. Franklin looked at her with confusion.

"Haley, is everything okay?" Franklin asked.

Haley took a while to respond as she came from her momentary drift from reality.

"Yeah, sorry. Could we cut today's session short? I just remembered I have to catch the pharmacy before they close," Haley said.

She grabbed her bag and stood up abruptly. Franklin stood quickly to follow her.

"Sure. Same time next week. Take care, Haley."

Haley flew down the hallway and went outside toward her car. She opened the door and slammed the door quickly. She looked at the passenger seat to see Alicia sitting beside her.

"I told you I don't want you in there at all. We agreed on it," Haley said sternly.

"You didn't tell him, did you?" Alicia asked.

"That's not the point, Alicia. I need to be there for myself. I can't be distracted with by you sitting there with me," Haley said. "They're going to lock me up if they know I'm seeing you all day."

"I miss spending time with you, too," Alicia said.

"You know what I mean. I'm going to make this right. Mark my words," Haley said, turning the car on and throwing it into drive.

Alicia reached for Haley's hand before she could start driving.

"This isn't your fault," Alicia said.

Haley put the car in park. "It is. I blame myself. I told him I didn't, but I do. I'm going to make this right. I'm going to show you each day how much I love you. I didn't get my chance before, but I will now."

Haley drove out of the parking lot. She kept on glancing at Alicia even though she wasn't there for the rest of the world.

17

WHAT THEY LEFT BEHIND

THREE BIKES SKIDDED TO a halt at the edge of the driveway of the old home on Wilkins Street. The home formerly belonged to the Cardones; a family always believed to be too bizarre for their small town. After frequently gossiping over the unusual and secret child they kept hidden most of the time, the town eventually chased them away. They fled overnight. Despite how curious everyone was about their personal lives, no one was brave enough to enter their vacant home.

That is until Ron and his timid friend, Chris, decided to conquer the challenge one afternoon. Their frequently taunting classmate, Vinny, followed them on his bike to the house, where they all boldly stood next to their bikes.

"Well, I've never seen you girls do something brave. Thinking about going in there?" Vinny asked.

"Fuck off, Vinny. We just stopped to look at what's left," Chris said.

"Such a pussy, Chris. What about you, Ron? Any balls in that little sack, or do you have a few years still until they drop?" Vinny asked.

"No, your sister got a big serving of my balls before lunch today," Ron said. Chris almost dropped his bike from laughter.

Despite how many kids Vinny picked on as a much bigger teenager, he frequently received comments on his rapidly developing younger sister, Anna. As hard as he tried, Ron and Chris still didn't tremble when Vinny tried to taunt them.

"Big talk for a little boy. Why don't you go in? Afraid the Biter Boy is going to get you?" Vinny asked.

"That's just a story. No truth behind any of it," Ron said.

Biter Boy was a nickname for Craig Cardone. Few people saw the young boy, but the few who'd had the rare opportunity to see him made sure the rest of the town knew who he was. He was often shielded with a modified muzzle. He had a severe biting problem that was often exaggerated.

Some families who had suffered the bites called him "Cannibal Craig' because they swore they'd seen pleasure in Craig's eyes every time he'd dug into their flesh. After the third bite, the family was given an ultimatum to have Child Protective Services intervene. The next morning, their home was empty, and they weren't heard from afterward.

Ron dropped his bike to the ground and walked toward the house. Chris flipped his kickstand down with his foot and ran after him.

"Hey, you don't have to go in there because Vinny challenged you. We don't know if it's safe in there," Chris said.

"I want to go in for myself. Vinny can hold our bikes up for all I care," Ron said. He looked at Vinny.

"I'm going in. Are you coming along, or are you too pussy?"

Vinny dropped his bike on the grass. "I'll lead you girls in. Come on."

Ron stood aside as Vinny led them into the vacant house. Chris hesitated at the door before entering. The house was what they'd expected. All the doors and cabinets were sitting ajar with some loose items still inside. They peered into the kitchen and the sink had a pile of dishes stacked next to it.

The refrigerator was open, with a repulsive smell lingering in the hallway. The bedrooms held nothing more than a few pieces of clothing and furniture. The bathroom had stains of old bathwater and the faucet was still dripping heavily.

"It fucking stinks in here," Vinny said.

Ron and Chris laughed as Vinny held his nose tight. They proceeded on toward the end of the hall, which had the drop-down attic door. Ron reached up for it.

"Ron, are you sure you want to do that?" Chris asked.

"I got to hand it to you, Ron. I thought you were the pussy. Looks like Chris is worse than you are," Vinny said.

"Don't worry, Chris. Once Anna hears how brave you are being here, she'll fuck you any day of the week," Ron said, patting Chris on the shoulder.

Vinny threw a fist at the wall. "If I hear one more comment about my sister from you two-"

"Relax. Why don't you go take a look for us?" Ron asked.

"Since you two won't, I will," Vinny said.

Vinny pulled the folding ladder down from the attic door. He braced the sides and climbed to the top. It remained dark as Vinny searched for the light, but found nothing. Ron and Chris noticed him trembling slightly and he climbed down quickly.

"What is it? What's wrong?" Ron asked.

"I thought I saw someone sitting up there, but it was only a shirt hanging from the ceiling," Vinny said, catching his breath.

"Oh, and we're pussies? Come on, we still have the basement to look at," Ron said.

They passed through the kitchen and looked at the littered food on the floor. They all gagged when they caught the smell of the fridge up close. Ron and Chris were smart enough to plug their noses right away, as Vinny couldn't help but continuously gag.

"Cover your nose, dumbass," Ron said. In the corner of his eye, Ron noticed a large wet spot on the ceiling in the kitchen. He suspected it was from a loose pipe, but the wet spot that leaked was a red-orange color. The puddle on the ground in front of him looked like a mix of water and blood.

"Hey, Vinny, would you say the shirt that was hanging in the attic was right about here?" Ron asked, pointing up.

Vinny noticed the wet spot and the puddle immediately after. "Holy shit, is that blood?"

"I think it is," Ron said.

"Maybe we should just get out of here," Chris said.

"In the basement together, or I tell the entire school, you were both pussies," Vinny said.

Ron grabbed the door and swung it open. "Half of the school wouldn't believe you."

The stairwell creaked and echoed a faint dripping from the cellar. The daylight from the kitchen offered nothing to the boys toward what lurked in the darkness below. Ron stepped on the top step, expecting a creak below his foot. He descended slowly, looking back to make sure his peers were close behind. Chris stood still on the top of the steps while Vinny glared at Ron, annoyed he'd stopped to look back.

"You going to pussy out this far into the house?" Vinny asked.

"Chris, you coming?" Ron asked.

"I really don't want to, you guys," Chris said.

Vinny let out a deep groan, annoyed that Ron expected anything more from Chris. Most encounters in school, and the occasional sighting at the mall, Vinny spent most of his time taking shots at Chris. As hard as Vinny tried, he never upset Ron, so Vinny spent all his time cutting into Chris. After a while, each insult got easier to deliver, since Chris never developed the tough skin Ron had.

"Go wait outside if you're going to be pussy," Vinny said.

"Shut up, Vinny. Chris, the house is empty. There's nothing to be afraid of. Besides, don't you want to tell everyone how you swept the house that Vinny couldn't do alone?" Ron asked.

Vinny extended his middle finger close to Ron's face. Ron winked back at him.

"Okay. I'll go," Chris said.

Ron descended again. Chris followed, and Vinny was last. The stairs creaked with the added weight of two others. Ron reached the bottom of the stairs while Chris held onto the railing for dear life, and Vinny impatiently followed behind Chris. Ron turned on the flashlight on his phone and peered around the empty basement. The little light from the dirty windows gave no clear sight of what was down there.

"Ron, turn the light on," Chris said, gesturing to the pull string dangling from the light above Ron.

Ron pulled gently, pulling the bulb to the ground and shattering it.

"Nice one, dumbass," Vinny said. "Just use your phones," Ron said.

Chris and Vinny illuminated their phones and followed Ron slowly. The faint sound of water dripping was the only sound the boys heard. They knew the leaking had been occurring for some time now, as their shoes slapped the deep puddles below their feet. Ron halted abruptly, nearly making Chris and Vinny collide with him.

"What the fuck, Ron?" Vinny asked. "I'm not trying to fall over in this gross basement."

"Look!" Ron said, pointing at a young boy leaning against the wall in the corner.

The boy's face was hardly visible, nor were the boys ready to approach. Thick rope was tied to a hoop bolted to the wall and connected to a collar around the boy's neck. Ron shined his light closer to the boy, showing dried blood all over the boy's mouth and nose. He didn't look awake or conscious.

"Is he dead?" Vinny asked.

Ron crept closer. Someone had taped a piece of paper above the restrained boy. Ron snatched it quickly and opened it up.

> *We always tried our best with our son once we found out about his condition. He required constant attention and restraint to stop all the mishaps and frequent biting. We know the problem will only progress as he ages and will eventually lead to people intervening. We will never forgive ourselves, and we will always love our son, despite his true nature. Let him starve. It's what's best for everyone. Don't let him out. -Melinda and Michael*

"They just abandoned him like some sick animal?" Chris asked.

"Worst goddamn parents I've ever heard of," Vinny said.

Ron dropped the note and knelt in front of the boy. "Hey, Craig. You in there?"

Craig was still. All three of them thought he was dead. Ron gently shook Craig to confirm.

"Craig, are you okay?" Ron asked.

Craig's eyes opened and, and he lunged at Ron. Vinny grabbed Ron out of the way just in time, pulling them both to the ground. Craig continued to reach for Ron, despite the collar around his neck digging deeper with every reach. The boys noticed the small bruises and cuts that Craig had earned with each stretch he had done for his duration here, and it frightened them. They all briefly pondered being left by their parents and quickly snapped back to reality.

"So hungry. Need food now. So so hungry," Craig repeated.

Vinny pulled Chris and Ron back out of reach of Craig. Craig continued to repeat his need for food.

"Those fuckers left him here to starve," Vinny said. "I can't say I blame them. He's a cannibal or something."

"I think the leak we saw in the kitchen was from someone being kept in the attic," Ron said.

Vinny realized the connection. "Fuck. I would've left town, too."

"What do we do?" Chris asked.

"I don't know. He can't be solely surviving on human meat," Vinny said as he walked over to Craig.

Vinny knelt in front of Craig, raising his hand to mouth level.

"Dude, what are you doing?" Ron asked.

"I want to see how hungry this little fucker really is," Vinny said.

There was no time between Vinny raising his hand and Craig biting. The bite latched and Craig tore through the side of Vinny's left hand. The flesh separated and Vinny fell back, gripping his hand, screaming.

Craig chewed his food quickly and swallowed it down. "So hungry. I need more."

Vinny screamed as he gripped his hand tightly, trying to stop the bleeding. Ron and Chris pulled him back out of Craig's reach. They leaned Vinny up against a nearby wall.

"That little fucker ripped my flesh. It hurts so bad!" Vinny yelled.

"Need more. Still hungry," Craig continued to mutter.

"Let's get him out of here and to a hospital," Chris said.

"On our bikes? Dude, our parents will kill us if they know we were down here alone. No way," Ron said.

Blood poured down Vinny's arm. The flesh below his pinky, that dangled from the bite, left a clear view of his tendons and bone. Vinny looked down at his hand, trying to contain his tears, fearing they would call him a pussy in school.

"He got you good, dude," Ron said. "What do you want us to do?"

"So hungry. Need more food," Craig said.

Vinny's pain switched to rage. He heard Craig's broken record sentence, even with his own yelling.

"So hungry. More food."

"Still hungry. Need more food." "You little shit," Vinny muttered. "Need more."

Craig's drool dripped from his lips. Vinny could see his blood smeared on Craig's face. He reacted quickly. Vinny stood and rushed toward Craig.

"Dude, wait," Ron said, going after Vinny.

Vinny got close to Craig, swinging his foot directly into Craig's cheek. He rolled back, hitting the wall. Vinny regained his footing and started driving his foot into Craig's gut. Craig, getting the worst beating of his life, kept repeating the phrases.

"So...hungry," Craig said in between breaths. "Need... food."

"Shut the fuck up, you sick piece of shit," Vinny said, drawing his foot back.

Ron grabbed Vinny, pulling him back, dropping to the floor. Vinny threw his elbows into Ron, trying to get him off.

"Chris, help me," Ron shouted.

Chris aided Ron in pulling Vinny to the ground. Continuing to squirm beneath their grasp, Vinny fought with all his strength.

"Let me go, I'm going to fucking kill him!" Vinny shrieked.

Ron held tightly and watched Craig sit up. Craig's face bled from a gash slightly below his right eye. His behavior seldom displayed any sign of pain or suffering. Craig touched his gash, flinching slightly, and pressed his bloody fingers to his lips. He licked down the thick drippings from his face and looked over toward Vinny.

"More please," Craig whispered.

"What the fuck did he just say?" Vinny asked. "Goddamnit, what the fuck did he just say?" Vinny jerked his head back, cracking into Ron's nose. Ron lost his grip as he reached to contain the bleeding of his own nose. Chris struggled to hold Vinny by himself.

"Let's just get out of here, dude. Quit acting like this."

"Fuck you. There's no place for you here," Vinny said as he spun around, driving his fist into Chris's stomach. Chris dropped to his knees quickly, gripping his stomach, unable to verbalize his anguish. Vinny stood up and walked back over to Craig. Still repeating his various phrases, he noticed Vinny and looked up at him. Craig eyed Vinny's gruesome wound.

"Need more. So hungry," Craig said.

"I got something for you to eat," Vinny said. He swung his shoe into Craig's eye socket. He let out a grunt and fell over, slamming his head on the ground. His eyes rolled in every direction while Vinny sat on his chest, raising his good fist to strike Craig several times. Ron collected his composure, wiping his bloody nose on his sleeve. He looked over at Chris, who tried to cover the flowing tears from his face. He still gripped his aching stomach.

Ron was ashamed to admit it about his best friend, but Vinny was right about Chris being too timid for this activity. Ron returned his attention to Vinny, standing to go stop Craig from a violent death. Vinny stopped swinging to catch his breath. Craig's left eye was swelled shut and the gash by his right eye, now ripped open wider, gave Vinny the hint this kid only needed the right amount of punishment.

"Where's my mommy? It stings," Craig said faintly from his swollen lips. Tears formed in his eyes.

Vinny leaned in. "Your mother isn't coming, you little fuck."

Vinny felt Ron's hand grip his shoulder firmly. "Let's go, Vinny. That's enough."

Vinny turned to look at Ron. "Take your pussy friend out of here. Let me put this sicko out of his misery. Leave now, or I'll start on you after I'm finished with the biter."

"Vinny, I'm not fucking around. Get up!" Ron yelled. Vinny tried to yell back, but pain pulled away all of his attention. He reached to touch his throbbing neck and felt the back of Craig's head. The sound of chewing rang in Vinny's ear as he tried to pull Craig off of him.

"Ahhhh!" Vinny yelled as skin and muscle ripped from his neck.

Ron grabbed Craig by his head and pulled as hard as he could. Craig's teeth chattered, trying to finish his meal. Ron fell back while gripping Craig and maintaining his distance, so as to not be the second course. Vinny gripped his neck tightly, but couldn't control the blood flow. He noticed Ron struggling to hold Craig and saw Chris looking on in horror, cowering all by his lonesome. His vision blurred when he noticed his hand and shirt stained dark from the flowing crimson of his neck.

He fell back, pulling down the rope that bound Craig to the wall. Craig swung forward toward Vinny, returning to his feast. Ron didn't know how much Vinny felt in his final moments, but he quickly got to his feet when Craig's last bite pulled the skin from Vinny's neck up toward his forehead, tearing it like wet paper. Ron pulled Chris by his arm and charged toward the stairs. Ron pushed Chris ahead of him on the stairs.

"Go out the front door!" Ron yelled. "What about Vinny?" Chris asked.

"He's gone," Ron said. "You're next if you wait any longer."

Chris dove up the stairs. Ron followed behind, closely. There was a loud snapping sound before Ron could clear the stairs. He looked back to see Craig had chewed through his rope. He wiped his blood-drenched mouth and bolted toward the stairs. Ron climbed faster, nearly toppling over Chris at the top. Ron swung the basement door closed and rushed toward the front of the house.

"What happened? Is he loose?" Chris asked.

"Go, get outside!" Ron yelled.

The basement door swung open. "So hungry."

Craig cleared the corner faster than Ron and Chris expected. Ron ran with all his strength, passing Chris.

"Dude, come on!"

Chris froze in terror, meeting Craig's hungry stare. Craig approached slowly, watching Chris tremble where he stood and letting his tears run down his face.

"Chris! Come on!" Ron yelled. He tried going back to grab Chris, but it was too late. Craig jumped on Chris, pushing him over the couch, and slamming his head into the coffee table. Before Chris could recover from the hit on his head, blood was already soaking into the carpet. Craig's aggressive feasting severed the flesh from Chris's shoulder. Ron met Chris's eyes, staring into the last horrified glare Chris would have.

His eyes rolled back into his head while Craig tore into the skin on Chris's chin. Ron backed away toward the door, trying not to make a sound. His efforts to stay silent, while drowning out the sounds of his friend's flesh being devoured, made his concentration wander.

Don't let him hear you. Get to your bike and go. The slurping continued, and Ron felt the door frame as he backed into it. Ron turned to see the door but returned his sights to Craig. Gripping the door handle slightly, he felt relieved. I'm going to make it out of this alive! He turned the handle. The door creaked. Craig stopped chewing and looked up at Ron. He didn't move, and he didn't blink. He stood quickly, angling himself in a stance that intimidated Ron.

Craig's speed had tripled since they'd first encountered him. Perhaps Cannibal Craig's family had abandoned him due to his inability to alter his behavior. Perhaps he was a lost cause. Once he got a taste, there was no stopping him. If his reputation was already that of the whispers around town, there was no telling what the Cardones had kept secret from everyone. Eventually, it would get out. Even worse, eventually Craig would get out.

"Hey, Craig. Listen, I really need to leave and get my friends some help. There's no need to get any more excited. You had a lot to eat, and it's time for you to relax," Ron said.

He turned the handle more, allowing the afternoon light to creep into the house. Craig continued to stare without moving. Ron pulled the door, allowing enough space to squeeze through.

"Easy now. I just want to help my friends," Ron said. He pulled the door open more.

"Not allowed to leave. Must stay and eat," Craig said.

Ron exhaled and swung the door. He tried stepping through the opening when he felt Craig pull at him. He could feel his shirt tightening as Craig bit at his sleeve. The skin on Ron's forearm broke, and he pulled his arm away from Craig, planting his foot on Craig's chest and kicking with all his strength. Craig flew back and hit the living room wall.

Without hesitating, he lunged, charging at Ron, chomping his teeth. Ron threw Craig down again and immediately bolted for the door. Swinging the door open wide, he was hopeful. Teeth dug into Ron's ankle, making him fall on his face and bust open his lip. He yelled.

"Craig, please don't!" Ron yelled.

Craig wasn't listening. Craig was eating; making up for the lost time his family hadn't properly fed him. No one was entirely sure how long ago the family had disappeared, but only three boys would learn they'd left their child behind.

I can't let him get out, Ron thought.

As his final endeavor to stop Craig, Ron threw his other foot into Craig's face, cracking his nose wide open. Ron stared as blood poured from Craig's nostrils, unsure of whose blood belonged to who. He reached down and pulled at the loose rope that still dangled from the child's collar. Ron looped it around the foot of the couch, tying a knot and pulling it as tight as he could. He smiled and felt better about his brief success until the bite on his neck gushed like a broken fountain.

Craig bit deeper into Ron's neck, ripping and exposing Ron's throat. Ron's mouth filled with blood. His back met the floor, and he looked up toward the open door, grinning as the daylight brightened the darkness that filled the house. Ron's blood dripped onto the porch and his last sight was the only part of him that would leave the house.

18

Return From the Depths

The sun beat down on the windy, backcountry road as Jeff drove toward the campsite. He tried to raise the volume as Dom couldn't stop complaining about his nightmare. Cassie and Luke nestled against one another in the back seat.

"Okay, tell me again what happened in this 'premonition' of yours," Jeff chuckled while looking at Dom. Cassie and Luke's laughter followed.

Dom shook his head. "I woke up and there was a woodsman standing at the base of my bed."

"A woodsman, you say?" Luke asked.

"Yes, a woodsman. He told me he looks forward to our camping trip, and hunting humans is his favorite. Then he stepped back into a black portal and vanished," Dom said.

The entire car, excluding Dom, broke into hysterical laughter.

"Go ahead, laugh it up. You'll be thanking me for the warning when you hear noises in the woods," Dom said.

"Don't worry, bro. Cassie packed extra bear traps and landmines. No way your killer woodsman is getting anywhere near us," Jeff said.

The laughter quieted and Dom pouted while gazing out the window.

"How much longer until we get to the site, Jeff?" Luke asked.

"Hopefully soon. I can't wait to get that tent set up," Cassie said while smirking at Luke.

"We all agreed to take this camping trip every year since the summer before college," Jeff said. "Can you two please cool it with the hormones? You're worse than teenage boys."

Luke and Cassie rolled their eyes before embracing in a passionate kiss. Jeff nudged Dom, who was still pouting. Dom looked over to see Jeff pull out a Roman Candle from the driver's side door.

"If they can't stop fucking, maybe this will give them a hint," Jeff whispered.

"How many of those do you have?" Dom asked.

"I picked up a few at that gas station. It's safe to say they didn't notice with all the PDA," Jeff whispered. "Let's scare them when they think they're safe."

Dom nodded and peered back out the window. Jeff looked in the rearview mirror to see Cassie and Luke going at it again. He shook his head in disbelief and paid attention to the journey ahead. It was another hour before the group reached the campsite. Dom got out immediately and ran toward the nearest tree.

"Holy shit, I have to piss."

"I told you, it feels heavenly when you wait for that initial burst," Jeff said, smiling.

"You're just too goddamn stubborn to go to a rest stop," Dom said.

Luke got out and opened the trunk. He pulled out his and Cassie's bags immediately. Cassie pulled him to the side of the truck.

"Let's get that tent set up first thing so we can pull it down," Cassie said.

Before Luke could respond, he felt Jeff's bag hit him hard in the back. He turned to see Jeff smirking.

"Oh, did I hit you? I'm sorry, sweetie," Jeff chuckled.

"Asshole," Luke muttered under his breath. Cassie and Luke walked off toward the site and Dom returned to the car to grab his bag.

"Why are you such an asshole?" Dom asked.

"Just poking the happy couple, is all. I'll signal you when it's time to fuck with them," Jeff said.

"Sounds good. Mind if I catch up with them?" Dom asked.

"Not at all. I'll be close behind you," Jeff said. Dom smiled before sprinting to catch Cassie and Luke. Jeff grabbed his bag from the car and closed the trunk. He reached for his phone in the console and closed the driver's side door. A young boy soaked in blood stood in front of the car.

"Excuse me, mister, can you help me?" the boy said.

Jeff dropped his bag. "Holy shit! What happened to you, kid?"

The boy started crying. Jeff got close to him to help and comfort him.

"It's okay, don't cry. Why don't you tell me your name?" Jeff asked.

"It's Bobby," the boy said.

"Do you know where your parents are, Bobby?" Jeff asked.

Bobby dropped his head and continued hysterically crying. Jeff tried to call one of his friends but realized right away his cell service was weak.

"Bobby, can I take you to where my-" Jeff started saying. He noticed Bobby's crying sounded like laughter. Bobby arched his head and let out exaggerated laughter. He held Jeff's face for a second before pushing him back.

"My parents are dead, and soon you all will be dead, too!" Bobby yelled.

Before Jeff could respond, a black portal opened behind Bobby and he stepped back into it, vanishing in front of Jeff. Too startled to wait to make sense of the experience, Jeff grabbed his bag and took off toward the campsite.

Cassie and Luke were unpacking their tent and quickly assembling it, while Dom had dropped his bag and wandered the grounds for a moment. It had been a long time since the group got out there, since Luke and Cassie became so serious about their relationship.

Dom was hesitant about allowing Cassie to come along, but he knew the conversation would turn into an argument. The trio wanted to keep their tradition going, but Luke had other plans for them, allowing their annual testosterone-filled bro weekend to be intruded upon by his new girlfriend.

"Where's Jeff?" Cassie asked.

"He's coming. I wanted to get down here before it got too dark," Dom said.

"You left him by himself?" Luke asked.

"He's a big boy. Besides, he was the one who showed us this place. He knows it forward and backwards," Dom said.

Jeff came running in shortly after, dropping his bag and falling to his knees to catch his breath. The group looked over at Jeff, startled. Dom approached him.

"Hey, you okay, Jeff?" Dom asked.

Jeff looked up to see that he was scaring Cassie, and Luke looked terribly confused. He stood up and looked Dom in the eye.

"Just had the biggest spider I've ever seen on my shoulder. Can't stand those fuckers," Jeff said.

Dom didn't appear convinced by Jeff's answer. "Right. Gotta be careful in the woods."

Cassie and Luke continued building their tent. Jeff walked past Dom and started setting up his things.

"Do you want to tell me what really happened?" Dom asked as he approached Jeff and huddled nearby.

"I just told you. I think it was a wolf spider," Jeff said.

"Come on, dude. They're talking about fucking and can't hear us," Dom said.

Jeff looked over to see that Dom was right. Cassie and Luke were whispering while barely assembling their tent. He watched as they backtracked through the correct assembly and continued to shoot each other flirtatious glances.

"I just saw a little kid, soaked in blood, step back into a portal," Jeff said. He thought Dom would burst into laughter like he had after the words left his own lips. Dom's eyes widened instead.

"Holy shit. See? I told you! It was a premonition or something. Maybe the woodsman and the little boy knew each other," Dom said.

"I won't get worked up about it yet. I think it's weird we both saw something similar with a haunting message. Let's just try to forget about it," Jeff said.

"What did he say to you?" Dom asked.

"He said, 'Soon you will all be dead'. Let's try to have a great time while we're out here and not worry."

"No, we have to talk about this. I cannot bottle this awful coincidence," Dom said.

"Hey!" Luke shouted.

Dom jumped while Jeff stood and dropped what was in his hands.

"We'll go grab some firewood. Maybe you two want to put your tents up before it gets too dark," Luke said. Cassie chuckled at them as they both walked deeper into the woods.

"My guess is they will pull off a quickie when they get far enough away. Now, let's talk about this," Dom said.

"What exactly am I going to say to you? We saw something weird. Unless that thing appears again, this conversation is over," Jeff said.

The black portal appeared in front of them. Neither of them could talk. Both expected a bloody young boy and a woodsman to appear next to each other. Nothing happened, except for the black portal hovering in front of them. Then their reflections appeared in the portal. Jeff's reflection coughed up blood and vomit. Dom's reflection bled from his eyes.

"No, no, no! Stop it!" Dom yelled.

Jeff covered his eyes. "This isn't real. This isn't happening!"

The laughter that came from the chilling little boy earlier echoed out of the black portal like a siren in the distance. Jeff looked to see the little boy sticking his head out, hysterically laughing. Dom saw the woodsman peeking his head out, smiling.

"It's almost time for hunting!" the woodsman yelled. The portal vanished. Dom and Jeff looked at one another, realizing that both of them had the same confirmation and fear about their experiences.

"We don't say a word of this to Cassie and Luke," Jeff said.

"Agreed," Dom said, as he saw the flirtatious couple return.

Luke dropped a pile of branches in the center of the campsite. Standing proudly, he waited for an approving response from Dom and Luke that he never got.

"Yeah, you're welcome, assholes," Luke said. "Don't worry, I noticed," Cassie said.

"I will get my tent finished. Why don't you sickening love birds start the fire?" Jeff asked.

Cassie and Luke shot Jeff a look that perfectly described their mutual disdain for his consistent comments. Dom finished his tent and Jeff finished shortly after.

JEFF COOKED AN ASSORTMENT of burgers and hot dogs over the fire as the group shared memories of previous visits to the camp. The sun sank deeper beyond the horizon and the fire became the only light source. Cassie nestled herself closer to Luke, as she frequently admitted being afraid of the dark.

"Aww, is Cassie getting scared?" Dom asked sarcastically.

"Fuck you, Dom," Cassie snapped back.

"Hey, just checking. It can be creepy out here. With the bears, coyotes, masked killers," Dom chuckled.

Luke threw his drink at Dom. "Dude, cut it the fuck out."

"Everyone calm down. Luke, why don't you tell Cassie the story of our first time here?" Jeff asked.

Luke smirked. "None of us knew how to start a fire. I doused the wood in lighter fluid and it splashed on Dom's shirt sleeve. His arm was on fire for almost twenty seconds."

"I had to get a skin graph from my leg. The memory is worth it," Dom said.

The guys chuckled for a little before growing quiet. Cassie remained silent since she was new to the group, only dating Luke for the past three months. Luke still gripped her hand tightly.

"Now we have someone else to make fresh memories with," Luke said, smiling at Cassie before planting the cheesiest kiss on her Dom and Jeff had ever seen.

"On that nauseating note, I'll go take a piss," Dom said.

"We'll be back out a little later. I want to have some quality time with the lady before I get too tired. Plus, some of us have a shot at getting laid," Luke said. He climbed into his tent after Cassie and smiled while zipping the door shut.

Dom shot Luke an angry glare before walking deeper into the woods. "Fucking asshole."

The light dimmed in Luke's tent and Jeff sat by the fire and poked it with a branch. He awaited Dom's return to discuss their portal problem privately. Jeff felt the hairs on the back of his neck stand up. Jeff turned around and saw the portal open close to his tent. The little boy stepped out, smiling with his mouth closed.

"I'm just going to ignore you since I know you're only in my head," Jeff said as he turned back to face the fire.

On the other side of the flickering flame, the portal and the boy appeared in front of Jeff. The boy opened his mouth and a mixture of crushed teeth and blood poured out.

"It doesn't hurt anymore. I wonder if you'll say the same afterward," the boy chuckled.

Jeff stood up and walked toward where he'd seen Dom flee to relieve himself. "Dom, where are you?"

Dom appeared from the side after Jeff called him. "Over here. Did something happen?"

"I saw that fucked up kid again," Jeff said.

"Maybe we should tell Luke and Cassie before something happens to them," Dom said.

Jeff shook his head. He assumed with Cassie's dread of the darkness that she wouldn't handle an apparition of that much horror. Luke, being the boldest of the three and trying to show off to impress Cassie, would assume they were teasing her and flip out. That, or Luke, would mock them for being pussies.

"I think you and I should figure this out on our own and leave them out of it," Jeff said. "Besides, they wouldn't believe us."

Dom shook his head. "What if something happens to them without our warning? Won't they point the finger if they find out we knew?"

"We don't even know what we're dealing with. Is it possible we have something in common that could alert this thing?" Jeff asked.

Dom pondered for a moment. He looked at Jeff, stunned by an answer that could connect them.

"I was thinking about that creepy old guy who lived at the end of my street when we were kids. Ned, I think his name was," Dom said.

"The guy found lying next to those corpses in his bedroom? That's weird, he. He came across my thoughts the other day, too," Jeff said.

Ned was a local who was disdained by the whole town, mostly due to his creepy appearance. Being someone of poor hygiene, and with the lingering gaze of a predator, he kept to himself whenever he had to be among people.

After several beatings from husbands who caught Ned's eyes gazing at their wives or kids, Ned learned to remain in his home for as long as he could, and go out only in the evening. Most kids who went near his house immediately felt his gaze from all points of the home. They frequently challenged one another to get closer and closer until they couldn't contain their fear of getting pulled inside for Ned's enjoyment.

After one or two people went missing in town, whispers and fingers all aimed their accusations toward Ned. When another three people vanished, police were knocking on Ned's door. When they found Ned soaked in blood, between several bodies stuffed in his bed and on the floor, the police tried to detain him before Ned's blade slid from his boot. It took ten rounds to get Ned to stop moving.

Jeff and Dom both suspected the same thought, despite how unrealistic it was.

"You don't think... Ned is maybe inside our heads?" Jeff asked.

"I really friggin' hope not," Dom said.

The black portal opened up in front of them. Before they could react, two arms reached out, pulling them close. The horrible face of Ned stuck out from the portal. They had both forgotten the awful smile that had made Ned terrifying until now. Ned's overbite, riddled with black and rotting teeth, extended closer to Jeff and Dom as he smiled widely at them.

"I have missed you boys. I have missed you so much. It feels like yesterday that I was gazing at you from my bedroom window, longing to have you over for a meal. Now, I can rightfully take you to my dwellings in hell," Ned said.

"In... hell?" Jeff asked.

"I made a deal to return. I searched the depths of hell so I could meet Him. He allowed me to return as long as I harvested my victims for his pleasure. I take their body and He gets their soul," Ned said. "The boy and the man in the woods were my latest to feast on.

Soon you will meet them here!"

Ned threw Jeff and Dom back and they fell to the ground together. Ned walked out of the portal. Jeff slowly slid back when he saw Ned's decomposing body approaching. Dom felt Ned's tight grip on the front of his shirt before lifting him up to his feet. Dom closed his eyes when he got an up-close glance at Ned's horrifying mouth of rotting teeth.

"I think I'll save you for last since you saw me first. I want to devour every drop of your fear before I finish with your body as my main course," Ned said. He licked Dom from the base of his cheek and stopped at his ear. Dom pushed away from Ned, falling back to the ground. Jeff got up and grabbed Dom by the collar.

"Come on, we're getting out of here."

Jeff didn't waste a second to stop and see if Ned was following them. He pulled Dom with him and kept running back toward camp. He heard Ned's faint cackling in the woods, but it didn't slow him down. He would try to convince Cassie and Luke to leave with them and explain it all in the car.

"Hey!" Cassie yelled. Dom and Jeff froze when they looked over to see Cassie standing at the edge of the camp by the trees.

"Hey, Cassie. Did we wake you?" Jeff asked.

"Wake me? Please, I probably put Luke to sleep, but I'm wide awake. Why are you both running like scared school girls?" Cassie asked.

"Thought we saw a bear. Turned out it was a raccoon," Dom said. He shot Jeff a look to reassure him they both weren't ready to say what they needed to Cassie.

Cassie walked up to Dom and Jeff. She slapped them both on the chest and they jumped back in confusion and pain. "What did I tell you about scaring me? Stop trying to freak me out. Listen, I have to pee. Can you guys keep an eye out without looking at me pee?"

"Sure, you got it," Jeff said.

Cassie walked into the dark to find a secure space to pee outside of visibility.

"Go wake up Luke and bring him over here. I'll watch out for Cassie," Jeff said.

Dom nodded. "You got it."

Dom approached Luke's tent with confidence that he would see the logic in their decision. He quickly opened the tent to see Luke's naked body lying down with his head back. Luke immediately noticed eyes on him and rushed to find some clothing to cover himself with.

"Woah, sorry Luke. Hey, I need to talk to you," Dom said.

"Dude, are you serious? Why the fuck are you checking me out?" Luke asked. He got dressed frantically.

"Checking you out?" Dom asked. "No, I wasn't doing that at all. Get dressed. Jeff and I need to talk to you about something serious."

Luke threw on his shirt and shorts. He stepped out of the tent and got close to Dom.

"Were you trying to see if Cassie was in here with me?" Luke asked. "I can tell you were checking her out the other day."

"Luke, I really don't need this right now. I'm asking you to talk to Jeff and me about leaving," Dom said.

"Then go get him and talk to me," Luke said.

Dom nodded and walked back to the woods to retrieve Jeff. He found Jeff pacing back and forth, waiting for Cassie.

"Dude, she's still peeing?" Dom asked.

"I don't know. She's probably finding a spot deeper in the woods, so we won't see her," Jeff said. "What did Luke say?"

"He told me to bring you over to the tent," Dom said, rolling his eyes.

"She knows her way back. Come on," Jeff said. Jeff and Dom walked back to the camp together.

After a few minutes of paranoid searching, Cassie found a wide tree in the deep woods. She normally wouldn't fear peeing in the woods, but she found it nerve-wracking to pee while her boyfriend's friends were close by. Cassie didn't believe they were creepy enough to get a glimpse of her, but she felt it was better safe than sorry at this point. She crouched down and relieved herself. She found the moonlight and dim stars calming as she tried to keep an eye out for lingering bugs and ticks invading her exposed legs and inner thighs.

A branch snapped nearby and Cassie jumped, pulling her pants up quickly. She turned to her left to see where the sound came from. A young girl stepped out from behind a nearby tree. She was in a pink floral dress, with braided hair draping past her shoulders. She was quiet, but she gave Cassie a friendly smile. Cassie walked toward the girl.

"Hi. What's your name?" Cassie asked. The girl remained quiet. "Are you lost? Are your parents nearby?"

A large hand, holding a butcher knife, emerged from behind the same tree. The hand swung down forcing the knife into the top of the young girl's head. Cassie gasped as blood poured down the girl's face. Underneath the blood, Cassie noticed the girl was still smiling.

"It's okay, it doesn't hurt where I go," the girl said.

Cassie covered her mouth and shook her head. "I'm dreaming. I'm fast asleep, and I'm dreaming."

Ned stepped out from behind the tree. He released the knife, and the girl fell forward on the ground. Cassie noticed his gross teeth and drooping, rotting skin.

"You aren't dreaming. I assure you, you're wide awake. I've come from another realm you might be familiar with. Where the dead go to burn and the demons feed on them. I broke the boundaries to return to my playground and harvest anyone I choose!" Ned said. "Once I show your little boyfriend what I can do, I'll feast on you all, one at a time."

Cassie ran toward the camp. Tears flowed down her face as fast as her legs escaped Ned's presence. She saw the guys gathered by Luke's tent.

LUKE LOOKED BACK AND forth between Dom and Jeff. After a moment of silence and contemplation, he chuckled. "That has to be the most ridiculous thing I have ever heard in my goddamn life."

"We agree with you, Luke. The fact is, it's true," Jeff said.

"So, this old serial killer has come back from hell to hunt us all?" Luke asked.

Jeff and Dom nodded in unison. They stared at Luke, hoping he will go along with their idea. Luke burst out in hysterical laughter.

"You guys are something else. First, Dom tries to check me out, and I suspect, Cassie, too. Now, you're trying to convince me of some boogie man who travels through portals? Cassie will get a great laugh from this. Where is she?"

Cassie came running out of the woods. Luke recognized her fear and hysteria as she ran closer to him and eventually collapsed into his arms. Cassie struggled to find words through her sobbing, sobbing and breathing deep from the strenuous run from the depths of the trees.

"Luke, we need to get out of here. There was this man in there with me and he killed a little girl. He killed a little girl right in front of me," Cassie said.

"What are you talking about? Did Jeff and Dom put you up to this?" Luke asked.

"Luke, I saw it with my own eyes. They weren't even near me. Please, you need to listen to me," Cassie said.

Luke pushed Cassie off of him and backed up with his hands in the air. He reached into his tent and pulled out his hoodie, throwing it on.

"This is great. Somehow, I missed the three of you ganging up to fuck with me. What is it, guys? Are you mad I brought Cassie along? Are you jealous I can maintain a relationship better than you two?" Luke asked.

Dom pushed toward Luke, getting in his face. "Fuck you, Luke. I don't know who you think you are, talking to us like that, but I won't take it. I'm furious you brought Cassie. This was our trip, our annual friendly bro trip for years, and you had to ruin it by bringing her along."

"Dom, please, I'm sorry. I didn't mean to get in the middle of you guys. I can call a friend to pick me up," Cassie said.

"No, we are in the middle of nowhere and it's not your fault Dom here can't get a girl. He has to throw it in my face that I somehow ruined the trip, even though I brought you along to show you how much this trip means to me. Dom, if you were man enough, you could have talked to me about this beforehand. But I guess that's too much for you, isn't it?"

Dom shoved Luke immediately after Luke finished talking. He stumbled back and caught his footing. Luke locked eyes with Dom.

"We can do it that way, too," Luke said.

He threw his fist into Dom's nose, dropping Dom to the ground. Blood rushed out of Dom's crooked nose, down his lips and chin. Jeff went to Dom's aid immediately and Cassie stood in front of Luke.

"What the fuck is wrong with you, Luke? These are your friends," Cassie said.

"Save it. Stop defending them, and stop playing along with their little game," Luke said.

A black portal hovered over Luke's head. Dom and Jeff noticed and backed away.

"Cassie?" Jeff asked.

Cassie noticed and backed up with them.

"So, this is how you're doing it? You're gonna turn on me for my friends? Well, fuck you, Cassie," Luke said.

"Luke, come here," Cassie said, without making eye contact with Luke.

"No, you are all assholes. I'll make sure you-"

"Luke!" Cassie yelled while pointing at the hovering black portal.

Luke turned to see what he didn't believe the group was talking about. He couldn't make sense of it, but he didn't fear it. As his friends and girlfriend stared on in fear, Luke looked on in fascination. The portal remained hovering, inactive, while the group stared up in anticipation of further torment from Ned. Luke, shaking his head, turned to Jeff and Dom.

"So, guys, where is your dreadful serial killer? He's awfully shy for being a homicidal psychopath," Luke said.

"You are the brave one, aren't you, Luke?" Ned said from inside the portal.

Luke froze in disbelief. Peering back at the portal, Luke knew he was the odd man out of this situation until now. Whoever he was about to speak back to, he knew their first message was correct.

"Look, I don't have a single clue what this is, or what exactly you want from any of us, but it won't scare me. So go ahead, do your worst," Luke said.

"Luke! Shut up!" Cassie yelled.

"Let's see what you can do to scare me!" Luke yelled into the sky.

"Very well," Ned said.

The portal ripped in half and dropped in front of Cassie. She looked on in horror as Ned reached out for her. Cassie's scream silenced as the blackness swallowed her whole. Luke ran toward it, hoping to grab her in time. He fell to the ground, and the portal closed both above him and next to him.

"Cassie? Cassie!" Luke yelled. "Where the fuck did she go, guys?"

"Ned took her. He's doing this," Dom said.

"How do I get her back? Help me, you assholes!" Luke yelled.

"What do you want us to do? We don't know what's going on either," Jeff said.

"Hey, bring Cassie back, you fucking piece of shit!" Luke yelled.

The portal reappeared, and Cassie stood in front of Ned. His bony, rotting fingers held Cassie's hair back tightly, making her cry hysterically. Cassie tried loosening his grip, but it didn't make a difference.

Ned pulled a large, rusted blade from his boot.

"Tell me, Luke. Are you brave enough to watch your beloved get scalped?" Ned asked.

"Why don't you come out here and handle me first?" Luke asked.

"What better way to handle you than to take the one you love?" Ned asked.

He swiped the blade across Cassie's forehead, separating her skin from the top of her head. None of the guys had ever heard a blood-curdling scream like Cassie's. Ned pulled back, ripping Cassie's scalp clean off of her head. Blood soaked down Cassie's face and filled her mouth as she continued to scream.

"I'll fucking kill you, asshole!" Luke screamed. He charged toward the portal, only to fall to the ground when the darkness vanished again.

"I am already dead. Killing your lady makes me feel alive, though," Ned said. His voice echoed from the still-hovering portal. The portal opened in front of Luke. Blood sprayed from inside all over him, soaking his shirt and getting on his face.

"LUKE!" Cassie yelled. The portal vanished.

"Cassie! Let her go! Please!" Luke yelled.

Jeff paced back and forth and Dom's tear-filled eyes stared on helplessly. Jeff approached Luke, putting his hand on Luke's shoulder. Luke turned around, shoving Jeff off of him.

"Get away from me! That's not helping!" Luke yelled. "Luke, she's gone," Jeff said. Tears filled his eyes. "Fuck you. She's here, she has to be here!"

The portal opened above Luke. Cassie's body fell from several feet, slamming down on the ground. Her lifeless eyes stared up at Luke and he stared back into them, ignoring the many stab wounds in her neck and chest. Her exposed skull, where her hair used to be, was hard to ignore. Luke was always a big fan of Cassie's beautiful brown hair. It was one of his favorite things about her.

The hovering portal closed. Dom cried harder, letting his emotions completely take over. Jeff tried comforting Luke again.

"Luke, let's get her in the car. We need to go," Jeff said.

Luke knelt in front of Cassie, looking into her eyes. He wasn't sad, but he was angry. He didn't want to give Ned the satisfaction of admitting it had scared him. Luke was angry and he would make sure Ned knew it. The portal opened wider than normal in front of Cassie's body. Ned stepped through, licking his blood-drenched fingers.

"Mm. A satisfactory sacrifice. A little treat for me and He gets a new soul to devour. Three to go. Are you next, Luke?" Ned asked.

"Let's see what you got, asshole. You don't scare me one bit. All you did was piss me off," Luke said.

"Luke, stop! Let's just get out of here," Dom cried.

Ned threw his knife at Luke's feet. "Show me, Luke." Ned stepped out of the portal and closed it behind him. Luke reached down to grab the knife and charged at Ned. With a heavy swing, Luke shoved the knife into Ned's chest. A mixture of black sludge and blood poured out. Ned stared down, emotionless.

Luke pulled the knife out and stabbed into Ned's chest again. Ned was still emotionless. Luke gripped the handle again, pulling the knife out and driving it into Ned's eye. Ned stumbled and swung his head back.

"How's that feel, you piece of shit?" Luke asked. Ned looked at Luke, smiling.

"I wish I'd met you when I was in my prime. Your anger would make you a skilled killer. Still, not good enough," Ned said.

In a swift motion, Ned pulled the knife from his eye and grabbed the back of Luke's neck, pulling his head back. Luke screamed and Ned shoved his knife into Luke's mouth and down his throat, leaving the handle visible for Jeff and Dom to see.

"That's two. One soul for Him, one bag of flesh for me," Ned said, smiling at Jeff and Dom.

Luke dropped to his knees, choking and spitting up blood. He tugged on the knife's handle, only to spit up more blood. He fell to the ground to be close to Cassie again.

"Come on!" Jeff yelled, pulling at Dom.

They took off toward the car, leaving Ned standing by himself. They didn't look back at all until they saw the car on the side of the road. Jeff ran toward the driver's side and unlocked the door quickly.

"Jeff, what are we going to do about Luke and Cassie?" Dom asked.

"We can come back for them!" Jeff yelled. "Get in!"

Jeff unlocked the car, and Dom pulled at the car door. The portal opened up behind him and Ned grabbed him. "Sorry, Dom, I changed my mind. Your time has come!"

"No! Jeff, help me!" Dom yelled.

Jeff turned the car on and put it in drive. "Hold on, I'll pull you!"

Jeff slammed on the gas. Dom held on to the car tightly while still being pulled by Ned.

"I've longed to have you since you were a boy, walking in front of my house. I won't let you get away this time," Ned said. He loosened his grip on Dom, reaching for his knife and thrusting it into Dom's arm.

"No! No!" Dom yelled. His grip loosened from the car and he fell back into Ned. They disappeared as the portal closed.

"Shit! Dom!" Jeff yelled.

Jeff sped off into the night, unaware of his destination or a plan to resolve his situation. He drove, quickly gaining speed, until he saw something faint on the road ahead. He slowed down when he realized Dom stood in the road, his chest bleeding. Jeff stopped the car and got out.

"Dom, what happened? What did he do to you?" Jeff asked.

Dom's stare lingered around Jeff briefly before they met eyes. Dom shook his head at Jeff.

"It's over. No one can beat him. Just drive and don't stop," Dom said.

"Get in the car, I can take you to-" Jeff said before he noticed something dangling from Dom's shirt.

"Dom?" Jeff tried lifting Dom's shirt and a mass of his intestines fell to the ground. Jeff stepped back while watching Dom try to put them back into his stomach.

"He wanted you to watch me put them back in," Dom said as he dropped to his knees, regretting those were his last words.

Jeff rushed back to the car and heard a strange echo. He looked around, seeing only darkness. He locked the doors.

"It's interesting, isn't it, Jeff? Three bodies, and I'm nearly capable of tearing through Heaven. Imagine what power I will have after you," Ned said.

Jeff couldn't control his crying. "Where are you? I just want to get this over with quickly."

"Look around. You're surrounded by darkness. See if you can tell where I am," Ned said.

"No. I don't see you anywhere," Jeff said.

"Drive, Jeff. I will give you more time since you are the final contestant," Ned said. "Call your mother, your high school crush. I don't care. Your soul belongs to Him now, and we will both feast by sunrise."

Jeff turned on the car and started driving. He looked toward the dark road ahead, terrified. He was unaware if he was already in the portal or not, but he made peace that his camping trip would eventually end.

19

A Final Clue

WEEKS OF CLEANING AND renovating the room after the investigation was over led to a new discovery. Deep under the floorboards, a hidden stack of papers was found. Crumbled and slightly torn, it was concluded to be the same handwriting.

This one was the turning point for me. I couldn't endure anything further, having been a victim of family abuse myself. Truthfully, I hope no one ever finds this one. No one should ever have to endure this...

20

Keep It In The Family

James shot up when he felt the wet bed all around his penis.

"Did I just fucking piss myself awake?" he asked himself. He pulled the sheets away, seeing his bare, flaccid appendage, drenched in his own secretion. His thigh peeled away from his fluids, still bound from the thick substance.

"Great, I guess I'm sixteen again." He had a habit of talking to himself when he was aggravated.

He exited the room, walking into the bathroom to peel his cum-filled boxers off his body before relieving himself. "Fucking lovely." After a quick shower, he exited the bathroom to find Damien creeping into the kitchen.

"Shit. Good morning, Dad," Damien said. He dropped his tense shoulders, realizing there was no point in hiding anymore. This was the third day in a row that James had caught his son either sneaking in, sneaking out, or making noise in the early hours of the morning. This time was especially weird. Damien was soaked from head to toe.

"Why the hell are you getting home at eight in the morning, and why the hell are you soaked?" James asked.

"I went swimming with... a friend." Damien wasn't very good at lying, and James usually saw right through it. There had been a slew of losers that Damien had brought home, mainly who clung to him like vampires, one guy after another. James had had it with these quick booty calls that his son felt were worthy of entering his father's home.

James's look said everything to Damien, but he didn't want to have this discussion this early.

"Dad, I met someone. A real person, with good qualities. Now, I know you're already thinking the worst of him because of my recent poor choices but trust me on this one. I mean it this time."

"Go take a shower and get some rest. I know it's summer break from college, but you also need to keep your head on your shoulders if you're going to keep your job for two months."

Damien walked into the bathroom without a response. He would convince his father later, and James needed to get to work.

The evening brought James and his exhausted body to the front door, with two pairs of shoes outside.

"Fucking seriously, Damien?" James said to himself. He didn't have the energy to meet this new destitute companion, nor was he awake enough to socialize. Damien was waiting at the dining table by himself when James entered.

"Dad, listen to me for a second and you can go shower and go to sleep. First off, I'm having my friend sleep over, and I promise we'll be quiet. Second, he's not quite ready to meet you yet. Now, I know that sounds—"

"Damien, that sounds like a fucking freeloader taking advantage of you," James said. His patience was already dwindling to the last drop.

"Dad, I'm an adult. It may be your house, but I ask you treat me like a man. If he's a loser, then you can throw it in my face. I promise."

"Just keep it down, please. You order food yet? If you do, get me a slice or two and leave it in the oven." James walked toward his room.

"Dad? I really think you'll like him once you get to know him," Damien said.

"For your sake, I hope you're right," James said, closing the door.

James's exhaustion kept him from paying closer attention to the ins and outs of Damien's new love interest. He caught glimpses in the early mornings, when Damien kissed his boyfriend goodbye, or saw the two of them standing by his car in the early hours before dusk. He thought it was best to keep his distance, trying not to ruin anything too early on. Damien wouldn't let his dad hear the end of it if it ever came to that extreme.

James frequently heard his son come in and out early in the morning for the next week. The initial entrance woke him up, but he went back to sleep. Upon awakening, one or two days a week, his soggy underwear was the first thing he noticed after opening his eyes. A grown man with no history of wet dreaming, was now experiencing it frequently.

"What the fuck? Not this shit again." He always snuck into the bathroom and showered to avoid crossing paths with his son, not wanting to come off as a demented pervert or something of the sort.

It reminded James of his estranged brother, Paul. He'd been a relatively normal kid until puberty. After that, James noticed his sexual behavior growing more and more abnormal. Masturbating at all hours of the day, sometimes even when their mother was in the next room. It wasn't until Paul made a move on James that he spoke up about his brother's deranged sexual cravings to their parents, which spiraled Paul into a deep depression.

He never emerged from the black void, and James hadn't heard from him since leaving high school. No calls, texts, not even letters after all these years, after moving out and hiding in a secluded lifestyle.

James feared it was some biological flaw that ran in the family. Their dad had been known to sleep around behind their mom's back, which is why she'd left him after finding the grisly details of Dad's perversions with women who would do anything he pleased. He hadn't shied away from recording them doing it.

Damien was more composed than Paul, so James tried to get his mind away from his estranged brother, leaving a stain on his naïve nephew.

Luckily, today was James's day off, so he was happy to sleep in a while longer, recouping from the idea of making his leg as sticky as a strong adhesive. He napped all day, except for waking to have a snack and a light lunch.

His dreaming was infrequent, but he did have one that stood out to him. His brother was at Point Pond, standing in the center, nude. His arm was bent at the elbow, and he stroked his cock, which dripped with mossy water.

James walked toward him slowly, also nude. His cock was flaccid, but as he grew closer to Paul, his erection stiffened. The brothers stood in front of one another, gazing into each other's souls like animals challenging each other before a vicious fight to the death. Paul steadied his stroking, reaching with his other arm to pull James close.

Their tongues met, swapping the same DNA from mouth to mouth. The brothers slurped each other's spit, passing it back and forth. Paul dropped to his knees, submerging his heavy body into the water. He took James' stiffness into his mouth, tasting what he'd longed for all those years.

"Just as I always wanted," Paul said, slurping his brother's pre cum. "As it always should have been, brother."

James wasn't normally one to feel an orgasm come too rapidly, but Paul sucked with intensity, and his urge to bust came rapidly. He felt his warm fluid fill Paul's mouth, and he fell back, splashing into the water beneath him.

He awoke to find himself soiled yet again; this time soaked with water, too. How the hell did I get this wet? The house was quiet, suspiciously quiet. James wrapped himself in a towel and crept by Damien's door. He was fast asleep in his bed.

I guess no boy toy today.

James rinsed himself off and got ready for an afternoon of running errands.

James came home and noticed another car in the driveway. Damien's boyfriend basically lived there at this point. Damien sat at the table, softly sipping at a chowder in his dish. He smiled once he noticed his father looking at him.

"Dad! How are you? I want to tell you something."

James could hear the shower running, and wasn't thrilled that someone his son was dating, who he still hadn't met, was already showering at the house.

"He's showering here now?" James asked.

"Yeah. We just got back from Point Pond. It's his favorite place to swim," Damien said.

Point Pond? Why there? Why there, of all places?

James tried to be polite about it. "So, he's a passionate swimmer? Seems like that's all you guys do."

"Yeah, something about being a good cleanser," Damien said. James couldn't shake his thoughts on the dream of him and his brother, only to hear about his son in the same place.

"Isn't there a pool at the rec center? You guys should go there," James said. "Besides, that pond can't be that clean."

Damien sat up, feeling the tension build in his father's tone. "He's done the research and assured me it's safe. We haven't had any issues yet. Plus, it's nice to rinse off afterward."

James didn't have any gripes about his son's sexuality, but Damien's need to discuss sexual details seldom made James pleased to hear it. He wasn't used to homosexuality, having grown up in a tiny town with a strict Christian population, but he loved his son, and it made him happy that he had the freedom James hadn't at that age.

"Damien, I can do without the details of your sex life."

The shower shut off. They both looked down the hallway. Damien shot his father a nervous glance.

"Why are you so nervous about me meeting him?" James asked.

"He's older. Your age."

James held his breath. He'd been quite vocal about Damien dating older men, finding it more and more disturbing each time he saw couples having large age gaps.

"You've got to be kidding me. Damien, you end this right now," James chided.

"Dad, just calm down. Give him a chance. Get to know him fir—" Damien's words were lost as he collapsed to the ground. James held him close, trying to get his son to wake from his abrupt unconsciousness.

"Damien? Damien!"

The bathroom door cracked open. "Well, I'd hope he'd still be awake by the time I got out, so I can formally meet you both at once. Now, I'll just say hello, long-lost brother." Paul stepped into the kitchen light, still dripping wet from head to toe. His towel was gripped firmly in his hand, dangling over his shoulder. His cock was stiff, pulsing with each step he took.

"Paul? Where have you been all this time? You're seriously still sick, fucking your own nephew," James said.

"I had to get to you somehow. You see, I distanced myself to find a cure for this. I thought I really was sick, wanting to fuck my brother."

James slowly placed Damien on the ground, rising to his feet.

"I thought I could kick the habit and live a normal life. I dated, and it helped, but I couldn't climax without the thought of you, inside of me or me inside of you. With that thought, I could cum over and over again."

"How did you find me?" James asked. "I changed my name to get away from you."

"I never stopped looking. I found your son, and he led me to you. I just knew it was fate."

James backed toward the kitchen. "Paul, you need to leave. I can get you help."

"I've already been helped. Did Damien tell you why I enjoy swimming so much?" Paul asked. He watched closely as James backed toward the kitchen, gripping something he couldn't see.

"I used to think it was for cleansing, helping me ease out of this gross idea of sexually pleasing my brother. After all this time, not letting it upset me anymore and embracing it, I see it as a way of purification."

James gripped the closest dish he could, tossing it at Paul. Paul caught it, like he'd trained to catch dishes as a profession. He smashed the dish into the wall, still firmly gripping a section in his hand. He squeezed with intensity, letting the glass dig into his tender flesh. Warm red fluid dripped to his throbbing erection, lining the length of his shaft with his own red lubricant. He threw the remaining glass at James. Paul stroked himself slowly, meeting his brother's eyes as his cock grew stiffer with his bloodied hand gliding from the top of his balls to the pink tip.

"No need to fight anymore, brother. We're all family here."

Paul swung his fist. James covered his face but caught the knuckles to his jaw first. His body went limp, and down he went. His last view was his brother's penis, dripping with a variety of fluids.

A heavy thrusting caught James's attention, slowly opening his eyes to the night sky. He was coming back from his brief attack, finding himself at the back of Point Pond. Cars drove in the distance, but even James's loudest scream wouldn't reach the street. The pace of the thrusting was accompanied by moaning, escalating in intensity.

Paul was pounding into his nephew mercilessly. He grunted as he slid his cock deeper, not caring if his victim was conscious or not.

"Paul, stop. Paul—" The urge to fight off his brother was stopped by the crippling pain in his limbs. James was contorted, bent like a fall victim. Both arms and legs were broken. Crushed. *How on earth did he do this to my body?*

"Once I'm done with your son's sweet asshole, I can please you like I've always been destined to. Well, at least this time while you're awake."

Those horrid wet dreams. It was all because of him!

James couldn't respond as his brother's moaning escalated. He thrust harder, trying to see if his son would survive this. Paul's cock pounded deeper. Formerly having a heavy-set build, James acknowledged his brother's ability to lose weight and tone up, growing to the size of a small body builder, although he wasn't using his new physique for anything good. James still had the height, and that's why he knew Paul wanted to please him as the smaller man.

Paul grunted loudly and with a swift pull, he quickly released his cock from the clenches of his nephew's anal cavity, pulling his anus into a prolapsed state. The agony shot Damien out of any deep sleep he had been drugged into, and he shrieked at the top of his lungs.

Paul continued to stroke himself. Damien's cry was silenced with the forceful press on his throat from Paul's foot.

"Quiet, I'm close. This will be a big one, too." Damien's sob intensified into a muffled scream. Paul's intense stroking came to a loud exhale as he coated Damien in white, splattering his face that had turned blue.

"Paul, he's going to fucking suffocate. Get off him!" James yelled, sending bursts of pain into his broken body. Tears filled his eyes.

"As I was counting on." Paul flicked his dick for the last time, pressing into Damien's throat until a loud pop silenced the three of them. "What a kid, but nothing like his daddy."

"Paul. That was my boy! You sick, incestuous, vile, piece of shit!"

"James, don't talk to your brother like that." Paul knelt between James's legs. He slowly slid them apart, trying not to cause further searing pain. He gripped his brother's cock, slowly stroking it.

"After all this time, we're still family. It's important to stay loyal to that."

Paul extended his legs, letting his feet soak in the water. James was stiff now, regardless of his urge to fight it. He couldn't counter the sensation of being stroked, and his brother admittedly was impressive at it. Paul swallowed his brother down with no warning, tasting his brother's shaft and massaging it with his tongue.

James withdrew inside his mind, trying to focus on his battered limbs and broken soul. He focused on his pain rather than his growing pleasure. Paul's determination was cutting through with each passing second. The pain was easing, and his release was building rapidly.

"Better than I ever imagined, James. Much better than your son," Paul said, before devouring his brother's meaty member again.

It came rapidly, without warning. Tears ran down James's cheek as warm fluids ran down his brother's throat. Paul could only let out a satisfied moan.

"I think we both owe ourselves a swim," Paul said, pulling his broken brother into the shallow water. James squirmed, even in complete suffering, dreading not being able to stay afloat.

"I can't keep myself up, Paul!"

"I'll keep you afloat, brother. It's the least I can do for finally giving me what I need." Paul dragged James into the water, clasping him in his arms. James shrieked in pain, but Paul's smile held firm.

"There, there, brother. I'll hold you close until you feel you can handle it."

James withdrew again, but the water, like his brother's incestuous grip, gave him no comfort at all. He hoped to be dead by sunrise.

Acknowledgements

To the many horror authors, I've met in the last two years who pushed me over the edge to get this book finished, thank you. I've encountered only kindness and generosity when trying to open the floodgates to my horrid imagination. All your support completely contradicts the terrible things you do to your characters, but I genuinely appreciate both.

To my family, both immediate and in-laws, that support all of my releases and simultaneously tell me I'm sick, I happily accept both. I'm afraid to release things at times, but the motivation afterward is worth it in the end.

To my friends who consume all of my content and tell me to keep going, I can't tell you enough how much I love you. I have a creative team that makes me feel immortal.

To my beloved Nadia. Despite how much time I spend staring at my screen and not shoveling snacks into my face on the couch in front of the T.V. with you, never forget that the little moments are why I'm so happy to have you and why I write. Thank you for the endless inspirational well that'll never run dry.

To my beloved parents who never gave up on me and always wish me well. I'm endlessly grateful to have your support. I would've never written a single word if it weren't for you two.

To anyone reading, new and old, you saved me from extinction. As a man who doubts himself frequently, knowing you took the time and the chance to read my words will go with me to my grave.

About the Author

Joseph has been writing since he was eleven years old. He was inspired by the Nickelodeon show Doug because he kept a journal at the same age. Since then, Joseph has written numerous short stories and found interest in writing screenplays.

Fast forward to his college graduation. Three short films written, produced, and directed with some film festival recognition. His love for writing stories, creating worlds, and developing characters to both admire and detest flourished as he never stopped creating.

Joseph branched off from screenplays when his ideas broadened beyond what the screen could portray. With a collection of stories in his archive and several novels in the works, there's no telling what will come from his mind and expand onto the pages.

With each piece of writing released, Joseph is constantly expanding his creativity while interacting with fellow writers, documenting his journey, reading, and filling his mind with more inspiration for the next story.

www.ingramcontent.com/pod-product-compliance
Lightning Source LLC
LaVergne TN
LVHW041704060526
838201LV00043B/564